CANYONS

CANYONS

a novel

Samuel Western

2015
FITHIAN PRESS
MCKINLEYVILLE, CALIFORNIA

Published by Fithian Press
A division of Daniel and Daniel, Publishers, Inc.
Post Office Box 2790
McKinleyville, CA 95519
www.danielpublishing.com

Distributed by SCB Distributors (800) 729-6423

LIBRARY OF CONGRESS CATALOGING-IN-PUBLICATION DATA
Western, Samuel.
 Canyons : a novel / by Samuel Western.
    pages ; cm
 ISBN 978-1-56474-574-3 (softcover : acid-free paper)
 1. Male friendship—Fiction. 2. Loss (Psychology)—Fiction. 3. Grief—Fiction.
4. Guilt—Fiction. 5. Revenge—Fiction. 6. Psychological fiction. I. Title.
 PS3623.E8477C36 2015
 813'.6—dc23
                          2015002586

For my darling Jess

I acknowledge, with gratitude, the help and support of the following: Anne Pendergast, Maryke Nel, my fellow hunting guides at the HF Bar Ranch, particularly Richard Platt and the PLAYA artists community.

All around me the dead
Accumulate faster than the living
And the light of their darkness is everywhere.
　　　　　　　　　—*Jeanne Lohmann*
　　　　　　　　Granite Under Water

CANYONS

CHAPTER 1

SKY CERULEAN AND CLOUDLESS. Cottonwood trees along irrigation ditches show speckled yellow leaves, waving slowly in a morning breeze, ready to make the leap to the ground.

In a field of barley stubble, two men and a woman in their late teens, shotguns at the ready, walk up behind a pair of quivering English setters. Ponytails on both men and patched blue jeans on all three. They walk roughly abreast of each other although Ward Fall, tall and erect carriage, strides slightly ahead.

Gwen Lindsay, slim, graceful, and favoring the long flowing hair of Joan Baez, walks slightly behind him and to Ward's left, awkwardly carrying a borrowed shotgun. Her twin brother, Eric, lollygags five yards behind, looking mildly bored, searching for a cigarette, while his two partners remain focused on the dogs.

A pair of cock pheasants burst from the stubble, flying right to left, cackling.

Ward raises his shotgun, but doesn't shoot, instead urges Gwen: "Take 'em both!"

The girl lets out a shriek of surprise and hurriedly puts the borrowed side-by-side to her shoulder. She pulls both triggers so quickly it almost sounds like one shot. The birds continue to fly. She lowers her gun slightly, laughing at her own ineptitude, relieved she didn't make a kill.

Ward swings and shoots once; feathers spin off the second bird, but it continues to fly.

Eric finishes lighting a cigarette, clacks the lighter closed, tucks it in his coat pocket, then raises his shotgun, also borrowed, and methodically takes both birds. Lead bird first, then the second pheasant. They tumble, beak over tail feather into the barley.

Ward, gun still half raised, stares at Eric.

"Damn, man. Second double of the day. For someone who proclaims not to care about hunting, you're doing some impressive shooting."

Eric breaks open the shotgun, removes both spent shells, and shoves them into his pocket. He shrugs, obviously unimpressed.

"Just luck. I've shot so many of these little bastards back in Nebraska it's almost second nature. Guess I'm over my limit now, aren't I?"

Ward waves his hand.

"No limits on this ranch, Lindsay. Shoot all you want."

Eric looks away, not knowing what to say. There had been times in the Sand Hills when, after another fight with his mother, he had shot twenty-five birds in a hour—a box of shells—hen and rooster alike, and let them lie where they hit the ground.

They walk to the dogs, who have run to the dead birds and are once again on point. Gwen picks up the first bird and places it beside the second, beak to feet, arranged so they look like a pair of women's multi-spangled shoes brand new in the box. She stoops, pulling back her long hair, studying the birds intently.

"I never get tired of looking at their coloring. Look at that shimmering indigo on their neck feathers. Cranberry, too. Aren't they beautiful?"

She shakes her head with wonder and a little regret, pats one of the dogs, then looks up.

"I'm starving, by the way. Is it too early to eat lunch?"

"Not at all," says Ward. "That wind is taking out the moisture we got last night. Makes it hard for the dogs to work a scent. I'm done. Your brother's done…I think. I told Celia to prepare a brunch for us around eleven o'clock or so. We'll be more or less on time."

"I'll carry these birds," said Gwen. "That's the least I can do."

THE OLD International half-ton sits parked at the end of an irrigation ditch under the shade of a lone mountain ash. Ward leans his shotgun against the tree and takes out a jug from the back of the truck and pours water for both dogs into a battered steel bowl. For a moment all three take pleasure in watching the dogs drink. Gwen sets the birds down in the back of the truck, hands her shotgun to Ward, then kisses him lightly on the mouth.

"I'm going to ride in the back with the dogs. I'll sit on that spare tire."

Ward looks a little crestfallen. "Don't you want to snuggle up front between two handsome hands?"

Gwen grimaces as she climbs in the back, calling the dogs.

"All you do is blather about philosophy and guys like Kant and what's his face? Hegel."

She sticks out her tongue in distaste and eases down onto the tire right in back of the cab and hugs both panting dogs.

"Besides, who could be handsomer than *these* two guys?"

Ward shrugs and shuts the tailgate. "We'll discuss nothing but art at lunch, okay?"

She smiles and gives him an air kiss. "Okay."

Eric walks around the front of the truck, shotgun broken and in the crook of his arm. He stands at the passenger side door, pulling the dead birds out of his vest and tossing them into the back of the truck. Ward sets down Gwen's shotgun, picks up his own, and opens the driver side door. As he reaches in to place the shotgun on the gun rack, he touches the trigger of the unfired barrel.

The birdshot goes through the rear window and directly into the back of Gwen's head. The force catapults her forward in a sparkling cloud of glass shards. She lands on her stomach against one of the wheel wells, the back of her head missing, her hair tangled with bits of skull. Ward reaches his hand through the glass in helplessness, cutting the back of his hand wide open. Blood and glass everywhere and the dogs bark crazily. Gwen's body rolls to the side and slumps on the truck bed, and her feet begin to kick like someone doing a frantic crawl. Then they stop.

CHAPTER 2

THE AFTERNOON SUN CUT THROUGH the palm trees, leaving narrow shadows on a sagging stucco rental. An aging silver Porsche 911 with nicks and dings sat parked under a metal-roofed porte-cochere. A half-mile away, the Pacific crashed on the beach. A block away, a backhoe leveled a house, a tear-down, the diesel undulating and surging.

In a back bedroom of the rental, Eric Lindsay sat at an open window shooting starlings with a pellet gun.

Shirtless, rail thin, and fishbelly white, Eric had gray, thinning hair pulled into tight ponytail. The room had no art and one bookshelf. An old acoustic lay on the made bed with a pen and a half-filled sheet of composition paper. A bedside tabletop held a worn Zippo lighter, a tin of best-grade Danish cigarette tobacco, a container of pellets, and an ashtray with a few butts. A hand-rolled cigarette put up a transparent plume of smoke.

A starling landed on a eucalyptus about thirty feet away from the window and began its screechy call. Eric shot him in the head and the bird fell like a stone. Eric took up the cigarette.

The telephone rang from the kitchen. Eric paid it no mind. Five rings. His answering machine picked up. The caller had a Midlands English accent, the voice tobacco-smoke rough and exasperated but also patient.

"Lindsay. C'mon. Pick up."

The speaker paused. Eric took a quick puff off his cigarette, put it down, and turned back to the window. He pumped up the pellet gun.

The caller continued.

"Something happen to you last night? I just got off the phone with Eddy. He said you never showed at the studio."

Another starling lit on the eucalyptus, this time a little farther away. Eric fired and hit the bird, but did not kill it. It tried to fly but flopped around on the ground. Eric did not shoot again, but watched it thrash in the underbrush. The caller continued.

"The mix is primitive, I know, and bad primitive at that. We've been through hell getting it where it is. Can't do the final without the overdubs."

There was a pause.

"Not going to bloody beg, Eric. You're leaving me no choice but to take you off first call for jobs like this. You want work? Lovely. Take a number. There'll be a long list ahead of you."

Eric did not look away from the window but spoke as if the caller were in the room. "Not as long you think, Graham. Not for that mess."

"By the way. You know who left a message on my machine looking for you? Yesterday, I think it was. Your pal, Hank."

Eric cocked his head and pursed his lips in exasperation.

The voice took a slightly more ominous tone.

"And, I believe I saw that refined luminary of kindness and understanding, Tavernier Alexander, sitting in his car across the street from my office. He looked like he was waiting for someone. That wouldn't by chance be you, would it?"

"Shit." Eric aggressively pumped up the pellet gun.

The speaker paused, then sighed. "Ring me by tonight."

He hung up.

A mitred conure parrot flitted to a tree within range and Eric instantly shot it; it fell, never so much as moving its wings.

THE SAME DAY, THE MK RANCH,
NORTHEASTERN WYOMING

WARD FALL sat in his pickup, alone but for the company of his blue-heeler, Mattie, at the edge of the rolling pine hills. He permitted his leather-soled boot to slip off the clutch, letting it resonate in the silent cab with a springy boom. He slowly cranked down the window and took off his hat and set it beside him on the seat. He was gray-haired and weary.

He reached under the seat and pulled out a bagged bottle of whiskey. He cracked the seal, flexing the purple scar that ran across the top of his left hand. Red wax scattered on the floor as he opened the bottle. He put it to his mouth and, feeling the burn in his esophagus, listened to the song of good whiskey gurgle down the neck of the bottle. He made a guttural sound of pleasure.

A mourning dove fluttered by, wings squeaking, a brave example of early migration. Ward watched a patch of spring snow slide from a pine branch with a rush, plopping to the ground. He drank again, deeply, then turned towards the dog.

"Wonder what they're doing at the other end of the property, Mattie?"

He answered his own question: "Doing their chores and asking themselves: Where's Dad?"

He drank again.

"Off having one of his spells."

He paused, staring dully out the windshield.

"Lorraine knew this one was coming on for at least a week. She's been looking into my eyes every morning. Looking."

Ward smoothed out a piece of paper taped to the dash written in his wife's plain block letters: SURRENDER IS NOT SLAVERY.

"Yes. Easier said than done, my darling."

Ward knew his skepticism was chickenshit. Augustine once averred that skepticism can only be overcome by revelation. "I'm still waiting, Augy baby," Ward once shouted into a welding mask while doing field repairs on a baler.

He took a series of gulps from the bottle, his veins now glowing, and looked at its contents, almost half gone. Despite the whiskey, he felt a chill and rolled up the window. He noticed snow being knocked off a series of trees across the draw. A young cinnamon-colored bear, back covered in shaken snow, clumsily moved among young saplings, overturning rotten chunks of wood, sniffing hungrily.

"Searching for sustenance," he said and drank again, but just a small sip.

The robins invoked the final notes of the day, that phrase they sing as the last residue of light slides away. He counted on their song when he was deep in some brushy draw looking for a stray. It meant he had ten minutes to get his horse out of the canyon. Evensong, he thought with some irony. It would be dark soon, but he had the light of the moon, swollen as a grape. Besides, a lack of light never prevented whiskey from flowing out of a bottle.

An hour later, with the moon climbing over the ridge, a woman dressed in brown coveralls, hat, and gloves, driving an ATV, lights on, slowly navigated the ground, following the tire tracks in the grass and patches of snow. She stopped when she saw the truck.

"Well," she said in exasperation, then softened. "Thank God he's okay."

Then she squeezed the throttle hard. The ATV jumped.

"Don't count your blessings quite yet, sister."

She drove to the truck, quickly shutting off the ATV, dismounted, uttering a quick prayer.

"O Lord Jesus, let him be just passed out."

Mattie whined from the inside the cab. She opened the driver side door and saw Ward slumped in the seat, breathing deeply. Whiskey bottle, almost empty, in his lap. The dog leapt down onto the floor, past Ward's legs, and out to the ground, stumpy tail wagging.

The woman breathed a sigh of relief, then came anger.

"Reduced to talking to the dog, eh? I guess she's the only one who won't talk back."

She took the whiskey bottle and dumped it out on the grass, then threw it onto the floor of the passenger side. She took off her gloves and touched his cheek.

"Oh, Ward. And you were doing so good. Must have been that dry spell we had before that snow. Well, shove over, mister. I'm not about to drive sitting in your lap."

She pushed Ward over to the passenger seat, struggling with his legs. He woke up a little.

"Lorriane," he said, groggily. "Sorry."

"I know. You always are."

He pulled himself over to the passenger side, pushing himself along the seat. Lorraine turned to Mattie.

"In the back, dog."

The dog vaulted over the side of the truck and scrambled in. Lorraine, short as Ward was tall, pulled herself into the cab and adjusted the seat. Ward crumbled into the corner. Lorraine shut the door and started the diesel. She backed up and headed down the way she came.

ERIC STOOD at the kitchen window, watching the flicker of Mr. Chou's television. His liver-spotted landlord lived alone in a spartan house devoid of womanly things.

Mr. Chou ignored the news and sat on the back porch watching his laundry drift in the breeze: yellowing T-shirts, white socks, and wrinkled boxers. Mr. Chou smoked, despite oxygen tubes running up his nose.

When the emphysema strangling his lungs took its final toll on Mr. Chou, new quarters would be in order for Eric. He didn't like to think about the task. Mr. Chou had sold both his house and his rental next door to developers; the title transferred when he died. Both were teardowns. "Don't expect any major repairs," Mr. Chou's daughter said when Eric signed the rental agreement the previous year. She handled her father's affairs and promptly came the first of every month to collect a check from Eric.

Mr. Chou and his daughter appreciated Eric for his solitude and tidiness. He earned their gratitude shortly after moving in when the main fuse shattered in Mr. Chou's house, leaving him in darkness. Eric drove to a Home Depot, bought him a new one, and installed it with Mr. Chou shakily holding the flashlight.

At dawn, right before sleep finally came, Eric often saw Mr. Chou going out for his morning walk, pulling his oxygen tank and cart behind him. Each month he moved slower.

Eric looked at the telephone, vaguely expecting a call from someone who would explain his quandary. The news that a collector for a loan shark and his ex-wife's attorney were both looking for him signaled that he had missed something. Not paid attention. A boomerang he had launched was coming back.

He checked his calendar in the kitchen and realized he had lost track of the days again. Besides studio work, he had no reason to leave his house. He ate one meal per day, usually around mid-afternoon. He disliked shopping, finding too many irritants along the grocery aisles.

A single shelf in the kitchen cabinet held everything he needed: coffee beans, a few good-quality canned soups or vegetables, dried beans, brown rice, and soy, the one dish he had learned to like at Berkeley. When ambitious, he would make a pot of beans with canned tomatoes and make it last a week. He would buy fresh fruits and vegetables a few times a month and eat them until they were gone, then go without. He felt sick when he thought about the marbled feedlot steaks his mother would serve. He had craved them at fifteen, though.

Occasionally old musician friends would try to coax him out for food and drink. He only rarely accepted and shied completely away from alcohol, which tended to stir up a hurricane of rage in his breastbone. And it did not recede after the wine was gone, either.

Thus, the days became a long streak without differentiation or name.

Eric liked best the almost quiet between midnight and four. He understood why Sibelius could not live in a house with flush toilets. He mostly worked at the Fender Rhodes, sipping coffee and smoking until the notes came, usually starting four or five at time. Sometimes the spigot would open and music came by the measure, so pure and right and fundamental, the one solid thing that no one could ever take away from him. He never hurried, even though the notes at times came faster than the pen.

He had figured out it was Thursday, and the conclusion added to his anxiety. A street loan he had taken out was two days over-due. That explained Tavernier. Eric could mollify the muscle if he showed him an ATM slip. The money—never spent it, in fact—was in the bank, of all places. He would have to pay the vig.

But what about Hank Yurio? Now what claim was that shyster inventing?

Eric rolled himself a cigarette and walked to the screen door. The darkening pink sky reflected off the back window of the 911. The last remnant of his old life and the source of his current money problems.

He recently noted that the Porsche was overdue for an oil change. Out of habit he dragged a magnet though the oil he drained from the block. Metal filings hung from the magnet like chain mail. It was a miracle the engine, forgiving jewel, still ran.

Twenty years ago he would have traded in the car for a new one and paid cash for it. Ten years ago he would have torn down the engine himself but now he had no inclination to do so. None at all. The one mechanic he trusted, who did not trust him, said he would need half in advance, half upon completion, for a rebuild. Cash only.

Quarterly royalty checks would cover it, barely, but they weren't due for nearly five weeks. The engine wouldn't last that long. He needed reliable transportation for those late-night studio gigs. Payday lender Lorenzo DuPree fronted him the $3,000.

The day before he was to bring the car in, the mechanic's wife called. Her husband was in the hospital having his appendix out. He'll be out in three days. Eric held on to the cash. Then a message on the machine. Infection, a minor one, she said, and her husband would be on the job within a week.

It was more trouble than it was worth to give the money back to DuPree only to re-borrow it five days later. On a whim, he stuck it into his savings account.

After Graham called he had continued shooting birds then walked to an ATM at a 7-Eleven on North Catalina to get an account balance. His heart skipped a beat when the slip that popped out of the machine read $4.28. Not possible.

He repeated the process. $4.28. There had been some sort of mistake made by those witless bean counters. He'd fix it in the morning. Walking back, he passed a liquor store with a window display for Bushmills. A craving arose for the slightly smoky flavor of good Irish whiskey. No, he better not.

He put out his cigarette and pulled out the ATM slip and looked at the date again. Still Thursday. Then the phone did ring. If it was Thursday evening a ringing telephone meant a call from the assisted living center in Valentine.

"Mr. Lindsay?" The voice of an attendant.

"Yes."

"Just a moment."

There was rustle of a telephone receiver transfer, then his mother's voice, strident and imperious even in dementia. She always sounded like she had just finished her sixth cup of coffee.

She cleared her throat. "Eric? That you?"

"Mom?"

"Well, it's about time you answered the phone. Go tell your

father to pick up your aunt Ula at the Greyhound bus station. She's waiting there right now. She just called."

"Hi Mom."

Then he waited. Sometimes he didn't respond to her imagined scenarios and her mind went elsewhere. Not tonight.

"Don't tarry. It's hotter than Hades and I can't leave the clerk's office right now. You and Gwen drop what you're doing and tidy up your rooms."

"Mom. Ula's not at the bus station."

"Yes she is. She just called. Don't argue with me."

"Ula's gone, Mom. Car crash. Twenty years ago."

"Car crash?"

"Uh-huh."

"When? Oh, yes."

She paused. "Outside Cheyenne. Am I right?"

"You're right."

Pause. "Gwen's gone, too, isn't she?"

"She is, Mom."

"She moved to California, didn't she? Left Lincoln. Transferred to your school. Am I right? To that hotbed of communism. Am I right?"

"Right." He knew what was coming next.

"You encouraged her to come, didn't you, Eric? I know you sent her the application and paperwork, telling her that Nebraska was nowhere. Don't try and deny it."

And she was off. It was *you* who had introduced Gwen to that *rich Ward-boy from San Francisco. You* were there when she was killed. *If she hadn't left Lincoln, she'd still be alive today. And saying sorry just isn't going to cut it.*

AT A crowded kitchen table, Ward Fall sat at breakfast with Lorraine and his three sons: Josh, age fourteen, and the two twins, Paul and Timothy.

Josh looked up. "Can I drive to the bus today, Dad?"

Ward took another bite of his ham steak and said nothing.

"Dad?"

"What makes you think you deserve the privilege?" said Ward. "I've seen little evidence that you're capable of such a task."

Lorraine glared at Ward from the other end of the table. He saw this, and tucked his head down, acknowledging that he might be out of line.

"Ask your mom," he said tersely.

"Mom?" said Josh.

Lorraine dipped her spoon into a jar of chokecherry jelly and smeared a dollop directly on her toast.

"Well, I think it might be okay, Josh. You've driven the tractor and hay truck hundreds of times."

"What about that accident with the AC?" said Ward, his eyes now on Josh.

"What? We've gone over this before," said Lorraine. "That wasn't his fault, Ward. You know that. Those brakes on that tractor would have gone out on anybody."

"But they didn't. They went out when Josh was at the wheel."

"I thought he handled the problem just fine," said Lorriane. "Besides, doesn't anyone deserve a second chance in your book?"

"Possibly."

"How possible?" said Josh his voice tentative, but not giving up.

"A statistically varying degree of probability."

"That means a 'yes' is possible. Right?"

The gruffness came back to Ward's voice.

"That means a negative answer is also in the equation."

"Oh, for mercy sake, Ward," said Lorraine. "The boy deserves a straight answer."

Ward glared at Lorraine, then at Josh. "Okay, goddamn it. Go ahead."

Lorraine dropped her toast on the plate and pushed her chair back.

"Ward!"

He ignored her and looked at Josh.

"If you fuck up, you won't get another chance for six months. A year. Understand?"

Josh looked at his plate: "Yes, Dad."

WARD SQUATTED beside the bucket of a rusting, idling backhoe, greasing the fittings on the bucket. He heard the Suburban coming back from the school bus run. Lorraine pulled the car beside the backhoe. She got out of the car, her swift, agitated walk revealing her anger. Mattie, sensing her mood, did not run up to greet her but remained by the backhoe, tail waving tentatively.

"Ward. For the love of God, what are you trying to do, crush that boy? Josh was so upset he didn't say a word the whole way to the bus stop. The twins sat in the back like ghosts."

Mattie crawled under the backhoe.

"Was it that obvious? Sorry."

"Obvious? Yes it was obvious."

Ward stopped working the grease gun and looked up. A rooster crowed.

"How'd he do?"

"Josh? Fine. Just fine. Was there even really a question he was capable of doing it? And get over this incident with the Allis-Chalmers. We all get in trouble. So what? It's how we get ourselves out that matters."

She paused, trying to cool off.

"I've been meaning to ask you. Have you told that doctor in Billings that your new medication makes you feel like shit?"

Ward shook his head, knowing he should have done something about it.

"Well, why in heaven's name haven't you?" she said, unable to calm herself. "Did you see the boys' faces at the table? Petrified, just petrified. No boy should be scared of his own father."

Ward nodded. "Okay, Lorraine. Okay."

Lorraine stepped back, signifying she had said her piece. "You going to try and find that pipeline leak?"

"I am." He began greasing again, holding the nozzle with

one hand tight to a shot fitting and pumping the handle with the other.

"I think I know where it is. Need to find out if it's a bad section of pipe or a seal that's gone to hell. You feel like checking the calves this morning? The grass is getting pretty skimpy. We really should put them on that lower state section today or tomorrow."

"Sure. I was going to saddle up Blue Sky anyway as soon as I did some laundry."

She started to turn, but paused.

"Ward? Have you thought any more about going to your reunion at Berkeley?"

Ward stopped working the grease gun and looked up.

"Why?"

"I think you ought to go."

Ward shook his head. "I don't know, Lorraine."

He set the grease gun on the front tire and stood up. Lorraine went to him and put her arms around him.

"You need to get out more, Ward. Get off the ranch and go discuss those things in all those dang books you have in your office."

"What's in those books doesn't mean much to me anymore. I think you want me to go talk to Eric Lindsay."

Lorraine nodded her head.

"That, too."

"No guarantee he'll show up. Probably won't."

"You'll never know if you don't go."

Ward broke away and moved to the other side of the bucket.

"I'll give it some thought."

She nodded. "Be back here for lunch?"

He nodded. "I think that's possible."

"Chicken dumplings. Don't be late, mister."

ERIC GUIDED the 911 into the underground parking garage. He slowed, looking in the rear view mirror, making sure the door shut behind him. The door panels flashed white as they went down.

He pulled the car into a slot and put it in neutral, listening to the engine. The valves clacked sharply, reverberating off the concrete walls, making them sound like an ancient sewing machine struggling to stitch thick cloth. The pitch hurt his ears. He turned off the engine and the lights. Under the dim fluorescent lights he made out a half-dozen cars, including a blue Montero Sport that belonged to the studio's recording engineer, Eddy Noyes. He didn't recognize any car that spelled T-A-V-E-R-N-I-E-R. But then again, there was no pattern to the man and no escaping him when he had his mind set on a visit.

There were no sounds but the ticking of the cooling engine, the squeaking of the leather seats, and the hum of the building and the traffic out on Alamitos. He tucked Graham's borrowed parking card in the ashtray and his keys in his coat pocket.

He ran his hands through his hair and sighed. He had numbed himself for tasks like this, rescuing the work of no-count musicians in sessions gone wrong. Some jobs were harder than others,. But the work paid well and, most importantly, allowed him to work at night and work mostly alone. It was also steady. The world produced no shortage of musical incompetents.

He reached under the passenger seat and touched the textured handle of the .40-caliber Glock, just checking to see if it was there. He knew himself a fool to tote around a pistol, a fool even to have it resting in a drawer by his bedside table, which is where it sat most of the time. But with Tavernier on the prowl and Yurio after him, the Glock's presence somehow served as a talisman, making him feel better. How could he have not seen this boomerang from Yurio?

As he sat back up, the dim bluish light darkened outside the passenger side window. Eric froze, wondering if he should try to reach back down for the pistol.

Tavernier's voice came through the window, muffled. "Uh-uh. Don't do that. I can get mine before you can get yours and then things will get ugly. Kindly open the door."

Eric hesitated.

"C'mon, Mr. Lindsay," said Tavernier, speaking in a slow, calm voice with a slight Carib patois. "Don't be discourteous."

Eric unlocked the door and moved a microphone case from the passenger seat, and Tavernier slipped in. He was a wiry, small-framed, toffee-colored Jamaican, favoring off-the-rack conservative suits and bland ties. He was always clean-shaven and wore a gray, banded fedora, a man you wouldn't think twice about if you saw him on the street. Insurance salesman maybe or actuarial.

Eric held the microphone case on his lap and Tavernier shut the door. He reached under the seat and pulled out the Glock, examining it. He extracted the clip, looked at it, then jammed it back in.

"You slyboots, you, Mr. Lindsay. My. My. .40-caliber. Fine piece of equipment, fine piece. Prefer the old .380 ACP myself. But," he said, hefting it in his hand and looking at Eric, "as I recall, the law says you aren't supposed to have one of these."

"And you pack legit? What the fuck do you want?"

"Oh my. I always make my social calls at one in the morning."

"I don't have the money."

"We figured that out already. What we want to know when you're going to get it."

"Don't know."

Tavernier shoved the Glock back under the seat. "Not the answer I was hoping to hear. But out of curiosity, what the hell happened? This is not your style, Mr. Lindsay, being late like this."

"It got garnished."

"It got what?"

Eric didn't feel like telling Tavernier a thing, especially not such an admission of idiocy. But he had to try.

"This engine," he nodded towards the back of the car, "is about to blow. Found metal filings in the oil. I couldn't wait another month for those royalty checks to arrive. The mechanic wanted half up front and half when he finished the job. So I came to DuPree—"

Tavernier interrupted, turning towards him, the pitch of his voice raised slightly to show his displeasure. "I did not come here to hear the details on financing your mechanical problems. DuPree wants to know if you got obligations elsewhere that he needs to know about."

Eric swallowed, his anger building. "Obligations? No."

"None? No sudden affection for nose candy or maybe you're making trips to the tables in Vegas?"

"Vegas? I got a writ of garnishment, Tavernier. The court took everything from my account, courtesy of Hank Fucking Yurio."

Tavernier furrowed his eyebrows. "Who is he?"

"Represents my ex. He convinced the court I've got unpaid commitments related to my divorce."

Tavernier shook his head, smiling slightly, and looked at him. "That's the craziest shit I ever heard, mon. Too crazy to make up."

Eric nodded.

Tavernier shook his head again. "Ain't that troublesome? You gone soft in the head though, mon, putting street money in that bank." He turned and, craning his neck, looked at the two guitars resting in the back seat.

"How much those guitars worth?"

"Some."

"Give me a number. You got more at your house, too, don't you? What's that you got in your lap?"

"It's an old microphone, not that it's any of your fucking business, Tavernier."

Tavernier moved his face closer to Eric's. He could smell a trace of English Leather. "You know something, Mr. Lindsay? You're absolutely right. It is not my business how you get the money. But it is my business to take care of business. Know what I mean?"

Eric pushed Tavernier away, instantly regretting it. He could feel the hard springiness of Tavernier's torso. The man never took his eyes off Eric's face but grabbed his left hand before Eric could make it into a fist. With his other hand, Tavernier seized Eric's shoulder and pinned him against the door. Tavernier scrunched the fingers together and expertly clamped them down like a vise. Pain shot through his knuckles and fingers. He winced.

Then Tavernier released the hand, as if he had second thoughts. "Sorry. That's your money hand, is it not, guitar mon? C'mon Mr. Lindsay. Be cool. Be smart. You're an educated fellow. Don't make yourself into a problem. You've got resources, no doubt."

Tavernier sat back in his seat, adjusted his fedora, and turned towards the door. He held out a finger. "And none of that cowboy shit, mon. I'm leaving that piece under the seat. I'm trusting you. You better not let the law catch you with that."

He opened the door. "You got 'til Friday. I need at least the vig. Have a good session. Who you recording for?"

"The Terrible Twins."

"How poetic. Never heard of them. Maybe I should ask my daughter."

Then he strolled to a nondescript Mazda and got in. As he drove out, Eric wondered where he got an entry card for the garage.

Eric sat back and took out his tobacco tin and fixed himself a cigarette, his left hand smarting as he rolled. His heart beat hard for a long time. That brackish taste now came on like a strong tide, fueling anger. To be approaching the half-century mark and be doing this. He was in the same financial straits as when he arrived in this town a quarter of a century ago, worse, actually. When he came to Los Angeles he owed nothing. At first the money from studio work trickled in. Then, before knew it, a wave swept him up: quarterly payments from song royalties and first-call studio work with legends. He bought a house, then another, followed by a fleet of Porsches, artwork, a guitar collection. He acquired an investment portfolio. Except for his guitars and the 911, it was all gone, whittled away by alimony payments and a $3,000 check each month to an assisted living center in Alliance, Nebraska.

He smoked until he felt the burn reach his fingertips, then he put the cigarette out. The last thing he felt like doing was redeeming music that was beyond redemption.

Eric clasped the handle of the leather-bound wooden box holding a vintage Telefunken and lifted it out of the passenger seat and stepped out onto the concrete. He took a deep breath. He had to quiet himself or he knew trouble would await him in the studio.

He gently set the mike box on the roof of the car and pulled the passenger seat forward and slowly eased the Stratocaster out of the back, careful not to mar the 911's leather interior. Then came the mud-brown bulky case of the Guild. After setting them both on the ground, he locked the car and looked around, half expecting to see Tavernier still watching him, tucked the microphone box under his arm and, making sure it was secure, picked up the two guitars.

Only one flight of metal stairs. His soft crepe-soled shoes and lightweight black moleskin pants made not a scuff or whisper. He wore an old silk shirt. Studio clothes. Nothing that would cause friction and sound. He moved in slow measured steps, no action that would allow him to hit something or knock the microphone loose from under his arm. At the top of the stairs, he stopped before a locked door, set down the Fender, and pushed the security buzzer. In a moment, he heard footsteps. Through the small window Eric saw a figure approach through a dark hall. A man in his twenties with spiked auburn hair and both ears pierced opened the door an inch. Eric did not recognize him.

"You Eric?" the man asked.

Eric nodded. "Hold the door open. All the way."

"Okay. Marcos," he said, introducing himself, opening the door wide.

Eric pointed his chin at the microphone box. "Take this. Use the handle. Don't drop it."

Marcos, who Eric assumed was a new sound tech, hesitated, staring at the box.

"Well c'mon, take it. I haven't got all goddamn day."

The tech nervously took the box, cradling it with one hand and slipping the other hand through the handle.

"Got it?"

"Yeah."

Eric released his grip with his elbow.

"What's in this?"

"An ELA M 250."

The tech raised his eyebrows and wrapped his hands around the box reverently. "No way. Original?"

Eric didn't answer but moved towards the studio, walking with quick, agitated steps.

"Eddy here?"

"Waiting behind the panel," the tech said, with the enthusiasm of a boy scout. "We got your isolation booth all set up."

"We'll need it all night."

"Really?"

Eric gave him a quick glance. "You listen to that tape?"

The tech shook his head. "A little. But this is my first week."

"A tech still wet behind the ears. Why did I expect anything different?"

They passed a series of dark offices, then reached the control room. The tech brushed past Eric to open the door.

Eddy Noyes, a heavyset man with bags under his eyes and a full curly beard gone to gray, turned in his chair. Miles Davis's *Sketches of Spain* crooned out of the control room speakers.

"Evening, Lindsay. You took your sweet time getting here, as usual."

"Took longer than I thought to prep for this job."

"Prep? What the hell you talking about? You'll eclipse these three tracks in less than an hour."

Eddy glanced at the guitars. "What's with the acoustic?"

Eddy then noticed the microphone box in the tech's arms and frowned.

Eric set down both guitar cases. He nodded at Marcos.

"Put the box down over there on that table. Easy."

He took out his tobacco tin, then hung up his coat.

"Need to redo some of these backtracks."

Eddy rolled his eyes, shifted in his chair, and glanced at the master recording and started to speak, but Eric interrupted.

"Who's supposed to take this recording?"

"Some independent is what I heard."

"They'll never take it, whoever it is."

"Oh really? Last time I checked, that was Graham's problem." Eric looked around in mock movements. "Graham's here?"

Eddy flashed a scowl.

"That's what I thought." Eric pulled out a cassette Graham had sent him. "You the engineer on these numbers?"

"Some, yeah."

"You tweak 'em?"

"Of course."

"Including the tuning?"

"Best I could. Ran them through the Auto-Tune."

"That spell-checker won't catch everything. Somebody needs to be horsewhipped for accepting this take in the first place."

Eddy leaned forward. "You sure you don't want to use a branding iron, Eric? Ain't that what they used on Hendrix and his engineer when he played out of tune?"

"I think you're just avoiding admitting you—or somebody—fucked up, Eddy."

Eddy stared at Eric and took a deep breath.

"Eric, c'mon, man. Relax. I ain't going to get into this. Leave it as it is, okay? This project's been a nightmare from day one. Graham's way over budget and we can't afford any extra studio time. The finished sound ain't your concern."

"Well my name isn't going on the list of contributors."

Eddy scoffed, his voice harder. "And when was the last time *that* happened? Graham resurrected this baby from the dead. Fact is, we've got to make the best out of a bad situation."

Eric handed the cassette to Eddy and made a whirling motion with his hand to run the tape.

Eddy put on the headphones, put the cassette in the deck, and pressed a series of buttons. He paused, then switched the control room speakers to a different channel. Miles Davis's sparse horn disappeared, replaced by an acoustic, out-of-tune guitar clumsily pounding out a three-chord pattern of E major, A major, and B major. The player botched the B major chord every time. Eric rolled a cigarette, listening. He lit up, inhaled, then let out a cloud of smoke.

"Enough."

Eddy turned off the tape.

"Can't overdub a lead to that. No way."

Eddy looked at him. "You can't or you won't?"

"Does it really matter?"

"The algorithm says the pitch isn't that bad."

"Eddy. Can't you hear that G string? It's almost a half-step flat."

Eddy cocked his head, half in annoyance and half in wonder. "Eric, how can you pick out exactly where the problem is?"

Eric didn't answer at first, then asked: "What's Graham's take on this project?"

"Said if the kid wasn't going to get it in six takes he ain't going to get it in sixty. Said he was sick of flushing hundred-dollar bills down the shitter, or the loo, as he calls it."

"We'll do another."

Eddy looked at the master sheet. "I don't think so."

"You planning to call Graham?"

"Not at one fucking thirty in the morning, I ain't."

Eric just looked at him.

The engineer shook his head in defeat. "All right, Lindsay. All fucking right. Have it your way."

"How about the two tracks with the rushed meter?"

"Did my best to salvage 'em. I punched in until my fingers were sore."

"Clicktrack broken?"

"Used it. The drummer still couldn't get it right."

"Christ." He opened up the microphone box and took out the Telefunken.

Eddy looked at it, studied Eric, then looked at the tech.

"I'll set this mike up myself in booth B," said Eric. "It needs to warm up. Need that special swing boom you have around here. For the lead, I'll want a Beta Fifty-seven up against a Fender Twin in the corner. You guys still have one, right?"

Eddy closed in his eyes and nodded and said wearily, "We got a Fifty-seven, Eric."

Eric walked out into the studio to set up the Telefunken.

The tech said under his breath, "So what's with Mr. Fucking Control?"

"Just do it, Marcos. I told you this wasn't going to be easy. You'll notice I didn't waste a lot of time arguing with him. He's got a hair-trigger temper that ain't worth pulling."

"Nice mike."

"Ain't no second best with Eric Lindsay. But you soon learn that nothing's ever good enough for him."

"Pale as sheet rock."

"Graham don't pay the man for his tan. Now get out there and set up Fender Twin."

———

ERIC DID not return to the rental in North Redondo. He knew he would lie in bed, smoking cigarette after cigarette. Trying to compose after salvage sessions was time wasted.

Instead he drove, in reckless disregard for the engine, north to Topanga Canyon. A reddish slit of light grew to the east over the Santa Monica mountains.

The house on Old Topanga Canyon Road stood unchanged. Same color. The kapok tree was a little bigger and there were a few new ornamentals out front. Someone had installed lighting along the walk. The grounds, what he could see of them in the dim light, appeared well groomed. The bumper of an Audi gleamed from the far end of the driveway.

Although he tried to tell himself that he was beyond such trappings, he missed the house and the life he'd had then. He'd written a lot of songs at that kitchen table. The music seemed to flow right through him. All he had to do was stop and be still and gather the notes as they passed, like collecting dried dandelion flowers in the wind.

Here is where it all went south, he said to himself. No. It didn't happen overnight, fool. The rage had always been there.

The brackish, brassy taste appeared in the back of his mouth again. Not a good sign. It presaged the emergence of his inner animal, a powerful force that, once in control, firmly held the reins. Eric recognized it as a precursor to trouble.

He recalled the time, years ago when living in Valentine, when his anger leapt to a new level taking on its own animal force. He had heard, then seen, the Chevy half-ton ambling along a two-track towards him. He knew the truck and its owner, a feed dealer's son who saw grease under his nails as source of pride and strutted around his truck in the school parking lot like a banty rooster. Three heads bounced along in the cab. A coppery taste ringed his mouth even before the truck stopped beside him.

The driver stuck his head out the window.

"Hey Lindsay. Thought that was your dad's truck back there. What're you doing way out here?"

"What's it look like?"

"Your game pouch looks a little thin."

"I'm not seeing that many birds."

The boy in the middle smirked. "I didn't even know you owned a gun."

"I don't. It's my dad's."

The boy in the passenger side window leaned over. "Hell, I didn't even know a smart fellow like you had time to hunt, all those hours you spend with that gui-tar or with your head in a book. You and your sister."

"Yeah," said the driver. "Hey, that sister of yours is developing some knockers, ain't she Lindsay?"

The boys in the truck glanced at each other and grinned.

Eric looked away.

The driver said, "If she'd ever come to one of the school dances, she'd be pretty popular. My sister says all Gwen does is stay home and fool around with her paintbrushes. What is it with you two? How come you spend so much time together?"

The boy turned and grinned at his companions. "Vice is nice, incest is best, ain't that what they say?"

When he turned back, Eric swung the shotgun barrel so it nicked the driver's lips. He held it there. A delicious, creamy feeling swept over him, almost like a wet dream. He felt supremely in control. The boy's eyes widened with shock, then fear. He immediately pushed himself back in the seat, grabbing the gun barrel, trying to point it towards the windshield. The other two boys scrunched down in their seats.

"Hey! Hey!" The driver said, his voice laced with panic. "Get that fucking thing out of here, Lindsay. Get it out!"

Eric held the barrel steady. "Take it back."

"Take *what* back?"

"Take back what you said about my sister. And take back what you said about her and me."

"Okay. Okay. I take it back. Both of them."

Eric pulled the shotgun away and the driver gunned the engine, spinning his tires in the sand, fishtailing, shouting, "Fucking weirdo."

Eric stood, not moving, glowing, awash with pleasure, that brassy taste fading.

In Los Angeles the trouble started soon after he arrived. The arguments with engineers and producers turned into shouting matches. Always the same thing: he could find fault with anything. Studios tolerated him because of his ear, arranging ability, and flawless sight-reading. Then came a fistfight with a rock star bass player who had taken Eric for a harmless skinny aesthete. Eric broke his nose.

His phone went silent for days. The songs stopped coming,

or rather they still came but nobody was buying. Divorce number two arrived. He remarried and quit drinking, hoping that would jump-start his career. Instead, the slow downward spiral continued. Desperation drove him to start peddling guitars. One by one they went, like ill-treated children whisked off by social services officials. He kept waiting for his luck to turn. Everyone said it would.

Alyson, his third wife, began ignoring him. Her career as a costume designer had the opposite trajectory from his. Always on the set. When he discovered her infidelity, he lashed her face-up to a long, narrow ancient Spanish oak table. The black nylon tie-down roof-rack straps kept her fully immobile. He gagged her. She was fully clothed, except for her feet. These he beat, slowly and gently at first, with a small beech club filled with lead, a priest, as the salesman at the fishing supply store had called it. He carefully limited his blows to the soles and never struck her with more power than his wrist would afford.

Two minutes of bastinado hobbled her for a week. The second time he beat her, she managed—she had seen him taking the straps out of a closet—to call the police. He was apprehended mid-stroke. She got the house on Old Topanga Canyon Road in the settlement, then promptly sold it.

He took the Glock from under the seat, taking sweet comfort in its grip. He did not like his simple life.

Pane by pane, he mocked shooting out the front windows of the house.

Boom. Boom. Boom.

He turned the Porsche around, angered he had made the trip, reopening bad memories and risking the car's engine. He rolled down the window and spat, trying to get that brackish, bitter, coppery taste out of his mouth. When he got back on Pacific Coast Highway, a wave of desperation flooded over him, that pressure in his head building. Despite possible trouble, he buried the accelerator.

Just as he approached the sign to Will Rogers State Beach he heard a high-pitched metallic rattling from the engine compartment. He took his foot off the accelerator. The rattling continued. He glanced at his gauges. Oil pressure held. Then the needle on the gauge ticked up, then plunged. He felt the hesitation through his foot, a small jerk, then, from the engine compartment, heard a sickening grinding sound followed by a loud pop. Next came a total loss of power. He managed to pull the car over to the side of the road, gravel snapping under the tires.

Although it was nearly daylight, he removed a flashlight from the glove box and got out. When he opened the engine compartment he smelled hot oil. His flashlight caught flashing glints of metal and oil all over the compartment. There was a hole as big as his fist on the right side the engine case. Dropped valve seat, probably. It could be anything, he thought.

He knelt and put his head all the way into the compartment, the gravel digging into the kneecap of his moleskins, trying to get a better look at the hole. A car pulled up behind him and Eric turned to look and saw the plates of a California Highway Patrol car. His first thought was how to explain why he was in the area of Old Topanga Canyon Road, a location he was to avoid, order of the court. Not a problem. He was plenty far away. As the first patrol officer bent down to look at Eric and ask about his problem, the second cop walked past on the right ride, flashlight probing inside the car. Eric heard his boots stop suddenly in the gravel and Eric knew the patrolman had seen the Glock.

"Sir, I need you to put your hands on the back of your head."

———

IN THE parking lot of the West Los Angeles police station, Graham and Eric climbed into Graham's black Jaguar. Eric carried the microphone box under his arm. His rumpled clothing and swollen eyes betrayed a lack of sleep. They simultaneously shut the car doors. Graham, unshaven, stuck the keys into the ignition, but did not start the engine. He took a sip of tepid coffee from a take-out cup and rested his head on the steering wheel, lifted it up, then turned to Eric.

"Martyrdom never suited me. I'm not sticking my neck out any further. No bloody way. This is the last bail-out, Eric, in any form."

"Said I was sorry, Graham. Installment plan on paying back the bail bond, okay?"

Graham started the car and backed up, looking over his shoulder. "Yeah."

He put the car into drive and pulled out of the parking lot. "Why not? Graham the sodding bank."

"My guitars better be in the fucking car."

Graham looked distracted, concentrating on the traffic on Santa Monica Boulevard.

"Which ones were they?"

"My blue 'sixty-three Strat and the Guild."

Graham grunted in appreciation of the possible theft problem. "I see. Well, honestly, Eric, I'd say you've got more serious matters to ponder than the fate of your guitars."

"Yeah, like what am I going to do for wheels?"

Eric looked at Graham and Graham back at him.

"What? Didn't I just say no more favors? Borrowing the bloody Jag is out of the question."

"Yeah. Yeah. Okay," said Eric deflated. "I'll buy a beater, I guess. Can't afford to fix the 911 now that Yurio took that money that DuPree loaned me."

Graham spoke slowly. "Let's see if I've got this straight: you can't afford to fix your car because the money you owe a loan shark was garnished by a lawyer who represents your ex-wife to whom you owe money. Have I got it right?"

"More or less."

"But you still own a $20,000 microphone and a $15,000 Strat."

Eric looked stonily out the window and said nothing.

The car pulled up to a stoplight. Graham turned to Eric.

"I was actually thinking not about cars or guitars but wondering how deep do you plan to dig your grave?"

Eric looked at him, puzzled, then flicked his hand at him, annoyed.

"What? Oh for shit's sake, Graham. No lectures. Please."

"Is Tavernier—or anybody—actually threatening you? Is that why you feel obliged to pack a pistol?"

"Yeah he's threatening me. It's not only Tavernier. It's just a feeling."

"What feeling?"

"I don't know, Graham, the future just feels bad. Got that black tinge."

"Sounds like same old same old to me," said Graham, his voice devoid of sympathy.

Eric stared at him, feeling that copper taste rolling into the back of his tongue. With a quiet fury he could no longer tamp down, he said, "Jesus H. Christ, Graham. Look at me. Look at me! I'm down to a rented shithole in Redondo, a house slated for teardown, and a dead 911."

"...And in possession of the most expensive microphone in the bleeding world."

"Not for long. Yurio put a lien on that, too."

Graham looked at him accusingly. "Keep going."

"What?"

"What you own...a 'sixty-three Fender and a late fifties–model Les Paul. What else? A priceless D-28—"

"That D-28's separate property. All the guitars are. The one thing my lawyer did right. They're all I've got left, that is. Besides, that D-28 belonged to my father. I fucking never should have told Alyson I had that guitar."

"Oh Christ, lad, everyone in L.A. knows you've got that guitar. How much does Yurio want?"

"Says I owe fifty grand. Still."

"And Tavernier?"

"Three grand plus the vig."

"And you think these incidents are related to the financial troubles of your divorce?"

Silence. They watched the palms whiz past.

"What the hell else could it be, Sigmund?"

Graham sighed and nodded his head.

"You're at a deadly spot in the road, Eric, a deadly fucking spot."

Deadly? Eric—no longer feeling so irritated but curious about Graham's tone—looked at him, a little wary. Graham was not a man given to hyperbole.

"Think so?"

"Your emotional litmus paper is about to turn very blue, it is. That's very fucking worrisome."

Graham took his right hand off the wheel and pointed toward Eric's heart, almost touching his shirt.

"It's when a creative man's ghosts are no longer content to hide in the closet. These demons emerge and rule with a rod of iron. Happens to blokes just like you. Success comes young. But then they lose their fire. They try to refuel themselves with booze or coke or pussy or slapping their wives around. But instead of going up, down they go. Way down. Can't count the number of artists who OD'd, or ended up in prison, or got shot or killed or died of fucking heart failure between the ages of forty and fifty. Marvin Gaye or that poor bastard Townes."

"Vodka and heroin killed Townes. I never made a pincushion out of my arm. I haven't had a drink in years, Graham."

"No, but you've got a meaner demon on your back, son. And I'd say you're right at the required six feet. Or deeper."

They stopped at a red light and Graham again turned to Eric. His voice got soft.

"Bottom line, Eric? I'm afraid I'm going to wake up some morning and read your obit in the fucking *Times*. That or being arrested for a triple homicide. Okay? If you hadn't phoned me to post your bond, I was going to call you this weekend and suggest going out for bite. When was the last time we did that? Me and you? I wanted to actually see your cadaverous self. Walking. In the fucking flesh."

Graham stuck a cigarette in his mouth, pushed in the lighter, waited until it popped out, lit his cigarette, then continued, his voice steady with conviction.

"You need a change of pace. Why don't you do a tour with someone? If the court says it's okay. Change might do you good."

Eric felt himself ease up a bit. Graham was the closest thing he had to a friend. "Graham. Thanks for the words of wisdom, but how about a cease and desist on this goddamn midlife career coach shtick. Okay? I'd rather get my teeth drilled with a dull bit than set foot on a public stage playing with musical morons. It's never worked. Never. You know that."

They stopped at a light.

Graham, however, was not in a mood to let up. With his cool cracking, he spoke in a low, acid growl.

"What *I* know is that you're bloody adept at pointing out the shortcomings of others but you have an arresting inability to hold a mirror up to yourself. Christ, Lindsay."

Graham let out a cloud of smoke. It came straight out of his mouth with the vigor of pressurized steam escaping from a leaky valve.

"You've spent the last twenty years pretending your world isn't slowly crumbling around you. Where's the bottom? That last step can be a bitch, you know."

The light turned green, but Graham waited for two women pushing a stroller to clear the grille by a good ten feet before he tromped on the accelerator. The Jaguar surged forward.

"When you drifted out of the sticks of Mendocino," he said slowly, keeping his eyes on the road, enunciating his words, "you had the luck of the gods. Within months you occupied a position that most musicians, *if* they're really lucky and *if* they work really bleeding hard, take years to attain. And here you are, closing in on the half-century mark, teetering on bloody bankruptcy, surviving on dwindling royalties, paranoid, out on bond for the second time in five years, pursued by loan sharks, living under a toadstool, and pissed off at the world."

Graham took a breath. "Have I missed anything?"

Eric waved his hand, motioning him to pull over.

"Thanks, Powers. I'd rather fucking walk backwards and barefoot to the impoundment garage than listen to this bilge."

Graham pulled over and held up a hand and, looking straight at him, said in a conciliatory voice, "Ah, fuck me. Listen to me. Sorry. Really, I'm sorry. Eric. Stay seated, will you?"

Eric took his hand off the handle.

Graham sighed. "Aren't you writing at all?"

Eric had thought about telling Graham about *Dreams of the Whippoorwill,* but not yet. It wasn't ready.

"No."

Graham saw that he had hit a nerve.

"I don't believe you."

Eric kept silent, then: "I got no songs worth selling."

Graham pulled back into traffic, simultaneously rummaging through his tapes box, and shoved a cassette into the deck. Aretha Franklin began belting out an Eric Lindsay song written nearly twenty-five years ago.

"The First Lady of Soul doesn't sing just anybody's bloody songs, you know."

"Ah, I know, Graham. That was just luck she bought that song—or actually Wexler bought it for her."

"Luck? How about the Mamas and the Papas? Or Tom Jones or Donna Summer? All luck?"

Eric reached over and turned down the music. "I've dried up, Graham."

"Is it that black and white? Over and done, is it? No chance for a rebound?"

"Not that I can see."

"Well, with that sun-soaked approach, I'd say you're about to begin the era of bankruptcy court, if not intimate familiarity with a prison cell. This handgun incident could cost you, Eric. Don't blow it off. A previous conviction of domestic battery, stricken or not, is not going to win friends on the bench."

Eric sat back in his seat. Graham also leaned back, a little embarrassed by the outburst, but obviously relieved to have said what he did. He leaned forward again as the car pulled up to the city impoundment garage.

"I'll beat it," said Eric lamely.

Graham shook his head, as if he was wondering why he'd bothered.

"Hope so. Hope you find your guitars. You want a ride back?"

"Thanks. I'll take a cab."

"Okay. Remember, the next royalty check belongs to me."

———

ERIC SAT on an armless dining room chair at his Fender Rhodes stage piano, working through a series of chords. The progression was in the key of C-sharp major. Seven sharps. Sparse and beautiful and ethereal.

Guitars in their cases neatly lined one wall, one stacked against the other like frozen quarter-fallen dominos. There was a small CD player and a turntable and a shelf of CDs and records. There were two amplifiers and a filing cabinet and a wastebasket beside the piano. Otherwise the room was empty. Eric methodically and confidently wrote the notes down on a piece of sheet music sitting on top of the piano. A single lamp lit the manuscript and his new notes. Out of the circle of light sat a small cardboard box stacked to the brim with completed songs. Cigarette smoke drifted about the room.

Eric reached the bottom of the page. Before setting it aside, he wrote *Dreams of the Whippoorwill con't.* at the top. He turned and opened the filing cabinet drawer to get another sheet of music paper. His eyes fell on a worn metal box in the back of the drawer. He took it out and rested it on his lap and hesitatingly opened it. A color photograph of himself and Gwen rested on top of a pile of photos and newspaper clippings. The picture taken at their high school graduation. Under the robe he saw the collar of a Nehru jacket that his mother so despised.

On graduation morning, she had stuck the keys to the Fairlane down her blouse to prevent them from leaving until he put on a suit coat and tie. Their father had already left in the truck, needing to check on the feedlot before heading for the high school. Eric had found the spare key hidden in the back of the kitchen silverware drawer. He made it clear to his mother that he and Gwen were going to graduation with or without her. She slunk into the backseat, sulking. She had been in a snit since breakfast when Gwen refused to tie back her hair.

Eric looked at the photograph longingly, something he rarely permitted himself to do, took a deep drag on his cigarette, then put the photograph back into the box and looked away but did not close the box's cover. Out of the corner of his eye, a bright yellow tri-fold pamphlet he had tossed caught his attention. He took it out of the trash.

University of California, Berkeley, Class of 1973 Reunion, it read. He flattened out the pamphlet on the keyboard, taking a drag of his cigarette, and read the whole schedule, flipping the pamphlet over. When done, he scoffed, but did not throw it away again. He stuck it in the filing cabinet.

He began digging through the wooden box and stopped when he found several newspaper clippings. They were yellowed columns from the *Wall Street Journal*, with the sub-headlines "Interest rates and bad timing cause collapse," and "Fraud and misjudging the mood of the Fed forces long-time California real estate dynasty into bankruptcy."

Another article detailed liquidation of Fall family assets, including the Ladderback Ranch in Idaho.

At the bottom of the stack was an obituary from the *San Francisco Chronicle*, headlined *Maria Henniker Fall 1926–1977*. It gave the details of Ward's mother's fabled life, noting her death in a private plane crash in Idaho's Sawtooth Mountains.

Eric said softly: "Doesn't that break my heart, Fall."

ERIC CIRCLED the edge of the gathering at the alumni house, smoking. Mottled sunlight passed through clouds, illuminating the graying heads of men and women talking of children and initial public offerings. A burning sensation began in the center of Eric's chest. It expanded rapidly, as if he'd swallowed a lump of searing iron. His solar plexus contracted hot, and for a moment he thought he would vomit.

The world's axis tilted. He drew frantically on his cigarette and steadied himself and was filled with remorse and contempt. He noted the red leaves of the cherry and could not, despite near vertigo, fail to recognize a reverse satori: instead of enlightenment, his moment handed him an illumination of error.

He forced himself to take in several deep breaths. The panic and pain abated but did not disappear. *Why the hell did I come?* he excoriated himself. He had nothing, not a single thing, in common with anyone standing on this patio sipping chardonnay or Anchor Steam.

Numbly, he turned out of the crowd, crushing the cigarette in his fingers. The pain helped him clear his head. He walked towards the shade of Strawberry Creek and stopped in front of a damp pink granite boulder. He sat.

He took out his tin of tobacco and papers, and rolled another, the fine shag floating to the ground. The water in Strawberry Creek gurgled in his ears. He lit the cigarette, then eased off the rock, brushing himself off, realizing it was probably the first time this silk suit had ever come into contact with an outdoor surface. Leather soles clicking, he set off towards the center of the campus.

Although he had not been in the Doe Library for twenty years, he remembered where he'd spent a lot of time: Philosophy, level B, Gardner Stacks. He got off the elevator, turned right, walked past the shelves, breathing in the stale air of never-opened books, then turned left against the wall, then right again into the heart of continental country.

Again, he caught himself asking why he was there. He hadn't read a line of philosophy in years. Was he trying to assure himself of his dislike of the subject, a feeling that began after Gwen's death? He remembered the near disgust he felt with classes he took in his senior year, marking time, but not wanting to drop out and give his mother the satisfaction of declaring he'd never make it through Berkeley, especially not studying philosophy and music.

Eric stopped short at the end of the stack when he caught sight of a polished, low-heel cowboy boot sticking out from behind a shelf. He stepped back and peered through the books.

Ward Fall was reading *Essays on Heidegger*. He was tall and stocky, about six foot-four, and had filled out considerably since college. Big, sunburned hands stretched across the cover of the book. Clean-shaven with close-cropped, almost monastically short, graying hair. His clothes were simple: boots, blue jeans, and a faded crisply ironed pink oxford button-down. Eric sucked in his breath, drew back, and stared at the spine of one of Schiller's early works.

A blur of rage shot before his eyes, shimmering and taunting. Judas library.

That brackish taste climbed to the back of Eric's throat. He waited for Ward to look up; surely he had heard his soles stop two aisles over.

His inner animal slammed its cage. Millions of pages about him, all trying to categorize the human experience. This was all in the head, isn't that what these cocky continentalists said? Perception is suspect, wasn't that your credo, Descartes, O prince of doubters? Experience, the least profitable exercise imaginable, was the ideology of the hoi polloi.

It all seemed so easy to swallow at age twenty. Went down like liquid silk. Now, standing in the library of a university named after a man who insisted that reality was concocted in the mind, such ideas scalded him with empirical gall. Experience drove a mean chariot. Nothing like a death to reveal the reality of the world.

To Ward, Gwen was nothing more than a novelty, a naïve hayseed curiosity, a supple prairie nymph who emanated a wonder about the world. He called her "my Nebraska Girl," but Eric knew she would be just one of his many conquests. He'd never given so much as a hint he'd grieved for her.

Ward looked up as Eric came around the end of the stack. Pronounced skin lines crackled across his face. Eric could see he was expecting someone, maybe even him.

"Still trying to decipher Martin, Fall?"

Ward's eyes rose to meet his.

"I think I'd recognize that pattern of footsteps anywhere. Hello, Eric."

He reached his hand out and Eric took it, giving it a quick firm shake, feeling the damp palm. Ward looked back at his book. It quivered in his hands. His nails were bitten to the point they no longer grew; the ends of his fingers sealed off the edge of the nail. He swallowed hard.

"I've been thinking about passages in *Being in Time* for twenty years. Sitting for hours in the saddle or the tractor seat I'd mull over parts. Thought I actually had it figured out."

He raised his face a little higher, inspecting Eric.

"But now I'm not so sure. You never liked this guy, did you?"

"Heidegger? I thought he was a nostalgic Nazi."

A film of anxiety crept across Ward's eyes. "Remember how we used to argue about him until the wee hours? What was your line, 'A reactionary can always be spotted by the things he wants to destroy?'"

"Did I say that?"

"You should know, Lindsay. You're the guy who never forgets anything."

"And you're the guy who never gave up trying on new answers. Should have known I'd find you here, still trying."

Ward nodded, looking uncomfortable, affirming this was probably true and a quest he should have dropped decades ago. He wiped his left hand on his pants. Small droplets of sweat began forming on his temple and the back of his neck.

"Why aren't you schmoozing with our peers down the way?"

"Probably the same reason you're not. We were never joiners, were we, Ward?"

Ward shook his head. "No. Not even then. No, if anything, we were the anti-joiners, members in the time-honored brotherhood of hermetic sages. But I heard somewhere you jumped the good ship of philosophy and entered the music world."

"The sons of Plato aren't much help paying the bills."

"Neither are the sons of animal husbandry, I'm here to testify. Has music been any more generous over the years?"

Eric shrugged. Larger beads of sweat began gathering on Ward's forehead and around his neck. He wiped them off with the back of his hand.

"You never had any trouble finding gigs," he continued. "Things seemed to land in your lap. I recall that time we were at a concert and that guitarist from that band passed out on stage. What was their name?"

"New Riders of the Purple Sage."

"Some guy you knew asked you to come up on stage and take the guitarist's place. You did it like you'd done it every day of your life."

"Right place at the right time with the right people. It's a different world out there now."

Under the damp across his brow, Eric watched as Ward's skin took on a gray pallor.

"Have I heard you lately?"

"Doubt it. What have you been listening to?"

"Same cast of characters. Beethoven. Schubert. Schumann. I've still got a few of your old John Coltrane albums. My wife likes country and gospel, though. Some of it is even tolerable. Seen you in a concert maybe?"

"Probably not. I haven't been on the road for a long time. All studio work now. You fly in from Boise?"

"No. Billings."

Eric was curious if he'd talk about losing that ranch. A dull patina of fear replaced the anxiety in Ward's eyes.

"Isn't that a long way from the Ladderback?"

"Don't own the Ladderback anymore," Ward said quickly, turning away as if to avoid a blow. Then he looked back and changed the subject. "Have a place in northern Wyoming now. How'd you get here?"

"Took the shuttle. My 911 died on me last week."

"A Porsche, eh? Have any trouble on the flight?"

"No. Left pretty early."

"You still with Candice?"

Eric shook his head. "I like marriage so much I've done it three times. You?"

Ward nodded. "Fourteen years with the same model. Have three boys."

"Three kids? Wow. Have any pictures?"

Ward smiled, then suddenly seemed very ill at ease, practically twitching. He reshelved the book. "No. Lorraine gives me hell for not carrying photos around. Look, I better be going, okay? I've got to run across the bridge for some errands."

ERIC SAT in the rental car—a Camry that smelled like solvent—engine off, windows down, smoking and shaking, sweating in such sheets that the pits of his suit went dark. A bead dripped from his forehead, traveled across the top of his glasses, and landed on the ash of his cigarette, hissing.

For a time after graduation, Eric had scanned alumni notes and occasionally asked a rare Berkeley acquaintance if they knew of Ward's fate. He waited for the announcement, he spent that extra minute paging through class notes to verify a black crucifix beside Fall's name. *Ward Fall was killed in a ranching accident*, or even better: *Man, long tortured by accidental shooting, takes own life.*

Gwen's death had set off a concatenation of sorrows in the Lindsay household. His father began staying home from the feed-lot, drinking coffee, listening to Sarah Vaughan and Ella Fitzgerald, smoking, always smoking, pack after pack of Pall Mall non-filters. About ten o'clock he'd switch to whiskey. Then about one o'clock he'd slowly drive to the feedlot. This went on for two years. His employers, life-long friends, kept him on the payroll, although he did no real work. Cancer invaded Ray Lindsay's stomach with speed and stealth.

His father's death so close to Gwen's put Eric's mother over the brink. Her vindictive streak worsened to the point of lunacy. Medi-cations, if she took them, made her tolerable; but she couldn't abide any of Eric's wives, accused them of taking her son away from Ne-braska. His wives said he was the same, a score and grudge keeper. He remembered every mean act against him.

As much as he wanted to think himself above such thoughts, Eric had to admit he still hated Ward Fall. Hated him for taking Gwen away from this world, hated him for his carelessness, hated him for retreating and never taking responsibility. Eric pushed the thoughts away and felt a quiet space form in his head. It had tak-en him years to develop this calming area, this softly padded den where he fled when thoughts of Gwen drifted into his brain.

The comfort never lasted. The anguish kept building, not dis-appearing, over the years. It was all right when he kept the lid on, but remove it and rage flowed like molten lava. He could no longer live like this.

CHAPTER 3

ON A SEPTEMBER EVENING, thermals swept the heat off the prairie and swung hot over the Powder River Breaks. They rattled the screens in the Fall home as the family bowed their heads at the dinner table. Before a meal of venison fajitas, Lorraine said grace. As she bent her head, a strand of her hair fell on her plate. She made no attempt to remove it until after grace.

"Heavenly Father. We thank you for these blessings and the food we are about to receive. We ask for these blessings in Jesus's name. Amen."

Ward looked up first and, as he did every day, took pleasure at the sight of his boys, all dressed in well-used utilitarian western garb.

"You boys feel like coming to Billings with me tomorrow?"

"Yeah," said the three boys enthusiastically, in unison.

Ward grinned. "All right. Your mother and I picked out a dozen cull steers that won't bring diddly when it's time to ship. We're going to hope for better luck at the Saturday sale."

"I bet we will," said Josh.

"Lorraine? Can you and Mattie cut out those sorry specimens we looked at this morning and put them in the small corral? Maybe one of the twins could help you on a horse and the other with gates."

"Sure. You want me to hook up the stock trailer, too?"

"Save us some time if you could."

"Be happy to. By the way, Ward. You had a couple of phone calls this afternoon."

"Oh?"

"Your brother had to cancel his visit next month."

The boys groaned in disappointment.

"Really?" Ward shook his head. "Remarkable isn't it, boys? A surgeon can't arrange his call schedule with the proper priorities. Saving people's lives comes before hunting for mulies. The corrupt ideals of the modern world. Who was the other person who called, Lorraine?"

"Eric Lindsay."

Ward put his fork down, his face and voice changing noticeably. "Lindsay?"

Lorraine nodded her head. "Yes," she said softly. "Paul, pass me a tortilla, please."

"What did he want?"

Lorraine broke the steaming tortilla in half. "He said he's going to be in Billings tomorrow night, playing with Garth Brooks."

"Garth Brooks?" Josh said, astonished. "Dad, you have a friend that plays with Garth Brooks?"

"Apparently so."

"He said he'd have tickets and backstage passes ready at the door," said Lorraine.

"Oh, Dad. Can we go? Pleeeeze," said Josh, who shot a look at his mother.

Lorraine lowered her eyes disapprovingly. Ward, breezy and happy only a minute ago, was now pensive.

"I don't know. I'll think about it, but don't get your hopes up."

Disappointment washed over the room and they ate the rest of the meal in silence.

WARD STOOD out on the back deck, looking at the early autumn sky, the Big Dipper so clear and bright. He thought about a quote from Ben Franklin he had memorized when still in high school:

When I stretch my Imagination thro' and beyond our system of Planets, beyond the visible fix'd stars themselves, into that space that is every way infinite, and conceive it filled with suns like ours, each with a Chorus of Worlds forever moving round him, then this little Ball on which we move, seems, even in my narrow imagination, to be almost Nothing, and myself less than nothing, and of no sort of Consequence.

Lorraine, in a nightgown, stepped out on the porch and took Ward's hand.

"Ward. Come to bed."

He squeezed her hand in acknowledgement.

"Are you worried about what Eric wants?"

"Yes."

"You don't owe him anything."

"I know, Lorriane. I know. Except fathomless contrition."

"You've been forgiven."

"God seems to have an easier time than I do."

"God loved David beyond measure, even when he committed adultery and arranged the murder of Bathsheba's husband."

"David also killed Goliath, not a twenty-year-old girl."

"Do you want to see him?"

"Lindsay?" Ward said slowly. "You know how bleak I felt after running into him at the reunion. Hell, I felt bleak before I went. Is seeing him this time going to be any different?"

"There will always be more questions, Ward, always. Why don't you tell him how awful you still feel about what happened?"

"I tried that twenty-five years ago. I'm not sure I've got it in me to deal with it again."

"It's there, Ward, you just have to ask. Why don't you go see him at the show tomorrow night?"

"I sure let the boys down at dinner, didn't I?"

"They'll get over it. I was thinking about going down to the colony. Mom called today. She's missing her grandsons. Maybe we'll spend the night."

"Why don't just the two of us go to Billings? Let's leave the boys with Don and Tina."

"Concerts like that make me uncomfortable, Ward. Not my type of show. But Garth sure does have a nice voice."

She took Ward's hand and led him through the screen door, sliding it behind them. She guided him to his side of the bed and eased him to the mattress, as a nurse would an invalid, and covered him with the sheet and light wool blanket. When Lorraine got in on her side, she lay on her back and took his right hand.

"Thank you, Jesus, for this day and the light you shine upon the world. Thank you for taking our cares upon your shoulders and looking over our family and helping us in our helplessness. Create in us a pure heart, O God, and renew a steadfast spirit within us. Do not cast us from your presence or take your Holy Spirit from us. Restore to us the joy of your salvation and grant us a willing spirit to sustain us. Amen."

WARD OPENED the door first, but Josh, dressed in clean snap shirt and pressed jeans, burst past him, boot heels clattering over the porch and down the steps. He strode to the truck attached to a trailer filled with cattle. He jumped into the cab and looked back at the house, adjusting his hat, twitching with anticipation. The twins, who looked sullen, came out with Lorraine and stood on the porch. Ward slowly walked down the steps.

Lorraine leaned against a post. "Boy, you look handsome. Think you can unload those cows without getting yourself covered in shit?"

"Mom! You better put a quarter in the cussing jar," said Timothy.

"I've got my coveralls and gumboots in the back of the cab," said Ward.

Lorraine walked to the bottom of the steps and put both hands around Ward's neck, cradling his head, her fingertips touching at his spine, and looked him in the eyes.

"Talk to him, Ward. Invite him here to visit, even."

"What would Eric Lindsay do out here? He's into Italian suits and vintage Porsches."

"You don't have to do anything. You could even take him hunting. Don't you have still those two land-owner elk tags?"

He looked at her curiously. Did she know what she was suggesting? He gave her a squeeze about the hips, then walked towards the truck. Mid-stride, he veered from his path, strode past the truck's idling diesel and cows banging around in the trailer, slipped into his office, and pulled a Forest Service map out of his filing cabinet.

As they drove, Josh stared out the open window, silent, his hat in his lap, the wind crashing back and forth through his thick black hair like young wheat before a rainstorm. Ward knew Josh heard at least some of the discussion about taking him to the concert. Such arguments left his son in retreat, stewing about the lack of consistencies that permitted common spats.

Ward saw in Josh his own struggles with uncertainty. At sixteen he had become enamored with the philosophy of Schopenhauer because the old curmudgeon knew, unwavering in his conviction, the answers to life's uncertainties. Josh had inherited Ward's inclination to find absolutes in the linear and sequential; yet he also had his mother's willingness to believe in the unknown.

Ward, too, had hated listening to his parents fight. Their battles had been pitched and virulent, especially towards the end. His father, brilliant as he was, was no match for his mother's unflappable conviction on how the world should operate.

He and Lorraine kept their quarrels to quiet questions and patient silences, although, when truly exasperated with him, Lorraine would make her feelings known no matter who was in the room. Josh did not know about the shooting incident with Gwen. How would his son react when he discovered his father's bleak deed? Ward could see that by calculus or impulse, or probably both, it was only a matter of time before Josh would figure out what happened.

Josh turned to him. "Did you know, Dad, that each rock on this road, each piece of gravel, down to the minutest piece of sand, even, is older than the oldest living creature on earth?"

———

A ROWDY and appreciative crowd packed the Alberta Bair Theater in Billings. Josh, his first time at a concert, stood tiptoe, enthralled. Spellbound. Halfway into the first song, he craned his neck, scanning the stage.

"Where is he, Dad? Where's your friend Eric?"

Ward had been looking, too, and at first concluded Eric wasn't among the musicians. Then he realized that the lead guitarist, the clean-shaven lean cowboy dressed like the Marlboro man, was Eric. This was the same man who not four months ago was wearing a custom-cut suit, oval glasses and $300 shoes. He looked happy to be in the shadow playing someone else's songs with perfection. Yet to look at him on stage, one might have guessed he'd walked right out of the bunkhouse for a Saturday night in town.

"That's him. That guy on the left with a tan hat. Right there."

After the concert, Ward took the passes left for him at the front desk and worked his way backstage. He found Eric alone in a dressing room, sitting slumped against the cement block wall. He rose to meet them both, hand extended and smiling. Ward marveled at how relaxed and calm he looked after playing for two and a half hours for 1,500 people. Ward couldn't do that. Eric looked authentic, right down to his packer heel Olathes.

"No Lorraine or your other boys?" asked Eric.

"Sorry. It was short notice. We couldn't make it as a family. Who picked out your duds?"

Eric shrugged. "Like these? I did. Just goes with the job."

"Thought you were done with the road."

"I thought so too, but the fact is I was perilously close to going to debtor's prison. My ex, for some reason, thought I should honor every penny of a fat pre-nup."

"Sorry to hear that."

"Me, too. Brooks's offer to work this tour seemed like the simplest way of getting the job done."

"When does this tour end?"

"About three weeks. We finish up in Indianapolis on the twenty-seventh," said Eric, taking off his hat and beginning to work at pulling his boots off.

"What are you doing after that?" Ward felt his heart thumping.

"Don't know. I'll have to count my pennies. I could use a break."

"How about Hake's Fork?"

"Where?

"Hake's Fork. That's where we live."

Eric glanced up briefly, his eyes questioning.

"What would we do?" he said, finally getting one boot off. "Attend cattle auctions and discuss feed prices?"

"Thought we might go elk hunting."

Eric glanced up again, looking like he'd been slapped. Then he carefully inspected Ward's face. He shook his head once. "Wow."

"Elk camp is a cool place, Eric."

Ward pulled the map out of his back pocket and dropped to his knees. There, on the faded and cigarette-burned carpet of the dressing room, he unfolded a new, crisp, green topographic map.

"We have summer pasture right up here," he circled a spot on the map with his finger. "Got a cow camp up in the Bighorns. There." He put his thumb on a ridge. "How about it?"

Eric's dismissive attitude and disbelief seemed to fade.

"Camping out, huh? Kind of late for that, isn't it? I don't know if my old bones would tolerate much cold or rough treatment. I'm an L.A. boy now."

"We wouldn't do all the walking. We'd use horses."

Eric looked at Josh. "He get to go?"

"Probably not."

"Your old man thinks school's pretty important, huh? I'd be surprised if it were otherwise. Horses and camping out. Sounds precariously wholesome. Thanks, Ward. Give me a little time to think about it."

THE NOTES would not come. Eric sat with his Guild at the kitchen table with composition paper and pencil. The table also held new books, *American Hunting Rifles* and *Elk Hunting Secrets*. The wooden box from the filing cabinet lay open, photographs and clips strewn about. Eric set the guitar pick down and again began flipping through the photos.

Gwen with Eric at about fifteen, sitting on the couch, him reading, her with her sketch pad, eyes flitting towards the camera. Two skinny kids; Gwen with Eric and their father sitting on the porch steps; Gwen riding her horse, Plume; Eric, with a three-quarter-sized Stella acoustic, up on stage playing with Ray Lindsay and the Western Wheels; he and his father wore matching cowboy costumes his mother made and insisted they wear; Gwen, with her easel perched atop a hillock, painting the shimmering grassy mounds that made up the Sand Hills.

Eric closed his eyes and tasted copper nails. He took up the pick and began playing Hank Williams's "I Heard That Lonesome Whistle Blow." He fooled with the chords a bit, shifted to a different key, then stopped and wrote down what he'd just played. Then he erased the notes. He played the riff again, wrote and furiously scratched out the notes. His breathing got shorter, shallower, and more rapid. He paused, played again, stopped, then suddenly stood and with both hands grasping the neck, smashed the Guild on the edge of the table, rosewood and sitka spruce shards flying to the floor, strings curling and flying when released from tension.

"Arrogant fuck!" he shouted at the plaster.

IN THE air-conditioned basement of a ranch house in Palm Springs, Eric looked over the rifles. The dealer, obviously former military, had asked a series of questions: Quarry. Weight. Physical Condition. Experience with firearms.

This was a strictly cash sale, deemed private, with no paper trail. Eric handled and hefted various models. It had been a long time since he'd carried a rifle. None of the models handed to him seemed to feel right or catch his eye. Finally the dealer left the room and returned with another gun.

He came back talking. "Like I said, from what I hear, elk are a tough animal and require a cartridge with hefty knockdown power. You've got a pretty small frame, though, so you might have to rely more on shot placement. Need to find that balance. And this...."

He handed Eric an elegantly simple rifle, stocked in lovely Circassian walnut.

"Might be just the ticket. Customized Ruger Number One, re-barreled to a .308 Winchester. Very flat-shooting cartridge. Sniper's favorite, and with the right load, like a 180 grain, it will take down anything you'll be shooting at. Recoil's not too bad, either, if the fit is right. Top-rated scope, too. A Kahles seven by thirty-six."

Eric took the rifle and put it up to his shoulder. His cheek immediately went flat on the stock and he found himself looking right down the scope.

"Sniper's favorite, eh?"

"Absolutely. Thousands of confirmed kills. How's that stock feel? Might be a little long for you."

Eric let the gun drop to his waist. Then put it to his shoulder again.

"Feels good."

"You say you have some experience? What's your grouping at one hundred yards?"

"I don't know. I haven't shot a rifle for a quite a while."

"You might think about spending some time at a shooting range. I can recommend some places."

"Thanks."

"You said you hunted when you were growing up. You ever use a single shot before?"

"Break-open shotgun. Old Sears and Roebuck, if I recall."

The dealer took the gun back from Eric and dropped the lever. "There's no safe way to handle a loaded falling block rifle like this. You don't have the luxury of being able to store rounds in the magazine and keep the chamber empty, like you can with a bolt-action rifle. A single-shot action means it's either loaded or unloaded. An excellent rifle, this Number One, but statistically speaking, it's been involved in more that its fair share of unintended firings."

He handed the gun back to Eric, who balanced it in his hands, marveling.

"No accidental shootings?"

The dealer immediately responded with conviction. "No such act. It's called negligence. An accident assumes that the person holding the gun bears no responsibility. From the instant a firearm is placed in an individual's possession, he's accountable for what happens next, no matter what."

The words sang through Eric like the call of wild birds.

The gun dealer asked him if he wanted some private instruction. Eric declined. With the exception of required private guitar classes at Berkeley, Eric hadn't taken any one-on-one instruction since eighth grade. He trusted intimately his ability to teach himself.

"Let me know how the hunt turns out," the dealer said in parting, his gesture more polite than sincere. Eric said he would, but he had no intention of ever contacting the man again.

He did not have to worry about money. He had sold his 1956 Les Paul Black Beauty. He hadn't played it in years anyway. Combined with the receipt from the tour with Brooks, he had paid off DuPree and Yurio, repaired the 911, and had enough left over to pay the rent indefinitely. He just hoped Mr. Chou would live at least a few more months. Eric cancelled his land line and bought a cell, giving the new number only to Graham and his attorney, who had managed to keep him out of jail. He could live without hearing from his mother.

He bought a bench-shooting rest, binoculars, range finder, and a cheap spotting scope. He forced himself to rise early and drive to an indoor rifle range. He liked seeing the Number One, bench rest, cleaning kit, spotting scope, and ammunition spread out on the shooting table. Clean and simple. The tools of the trade.

He gave his last name to no one. If he played it subtle and discreet, he would have no trouble carrying a rifle. He carried the gun in a vintage Fender case lined with ragged silk. He still kicked himself about the incident with the Glock. How stupid could he be?

At the range, his gun attracted praise from other shooters. Eric learned that the gun dealer was right: the .308 had a reputation as an ultra-accurate cartridge. Observation and discussions with other shooters taught him that even greater accuracy could be achieved with hand-loaded ammunition.

Some shooters offered to load a box for him. He barely had the will to resist the offer, so great was his curiosity. As with his association with the gun dealer, Eric wanted no obligation and, after the hunting trip, had no plans to return to the range.

He kept to himself and discouraged conversation. Other shooters respected his wish to be left alone. These men with guns, so obsessive about control, would never understand or forgive or trust anyone who'd been involved in a shooting with unintended consequences. They measured their targets with calipers and micrometers. Furthermore, Eric recognized how much he was like them; their quest for a perfect target differed little from his demand for a flawless recording session or score. Their world would hold him hostage.

Each day his shooting improved. He kept records of his marksmanship. Within two weeks, Eric was consistently shooting a pattern with holes three-quarters of an inch apart. A quarter could cover the entire group.

He studied hunting magazines and catalogs for suggestions on clothing and boots, feeling inept at having to read something to know what to wear. He didn't like relying on advertising, which is really what catalogs were, for equipment. Ward offered scant help when it came to details concerning gear: two pairs of boots, one smooth-soled for riding, the other "pacs" in case it snowed; Carharts; two pairs of gloves ("light and heavy," he wrote); a heavy and a light coat, preferably waterproof; hat, orange vest, long underwear, and plenty of socks.

An unspoken paternal assumption presided over this list that simultaneously pleased and irritated Eric. Ward thought him to be an urbanite incapable of owning any real hunting gear. He hadn't even mentioned binoculars or a gun. Did Ward really think him that inept?

This underestimation of his abilities gave Eric more confidence for the task that lay ahead. His own list included the best of everything he could find. He couldn't fully anticipate his needs, so he best ensure against the unknown. He purchased a pair of Filson single tin pants; a Gerber folding knife; a steel-blue Polarguard sleeping bag, pad, bivy sack; expedition-grade long underwear; and a pair of high-top sheepskin moccasins.

He spent a long time browsing for boots. His Olathes were made for riding, although they were a little tight. Ward's advice for foul-weather boots was overkill, Eric decided. The pacs Eric found in a catalog weighed six pounds. Instead, he bought a pair of silicone-sealed ankle-high hiking boots.

He unsuccessfully tried to cut back on his smoking; he took out a month-long membership at a health club. The monitor at the workout room raised her eyebrows when Eric tired after only seven minutes on the treadmill. She skipped any lecture when she found out he smoked, but asked him when was the last time he had a physical. Years, he thought, although he'd been checked out pretty thoroughly when he'd been involved in a car accident. But that had been eight springs ago. She recommended a full examination and told him to go easy.

CHAPTER 4

HE BRAKED THE RENTED FORD Explorer as the red dirt road wound around a curve. The road was located at the very north edge of Wyoming's Powder River Basin. All Eric saw, and all he had seen the last hour, were faded red buttes, barren and bald, with rocky draws full of bunch grass and sagebrush. He eventually stopped the car. Almost goddamn desert, he thought, but not quite; and he studied Ward's hand-drawn map.

Eric sucked on his cigarette, then extinguished it. He rolled down the window and shut off the engine. Hot Indian summer air and swirling dust blew around his face. Occasional droughts in Nebraska had given him a hatred of dust, and this startlingly bleak land had it in spades. He hadn't been at Berkeley a week before he'd driven to the Albany mudflats and was bowled over by the smell, the layered, complex, textured richness of a mudflat at low tide. It made Nebraska seem sterile.

He thought he was in Wyoming, but it could just as well be Montana. The road seemed to wander back and forth over the state line like an aimless sparrow. He'd lost what natural sense of direction he ever had in his youth and now required a street sign to know where he was. Flying into Billings, he was surprised at its size, but then he saw how blackness spread around the city the way endless electric light surrounded Los Angeles. The outskirts of Billings dwindled off into individual splotches of white, like the lights of anchored ships in a harbor, then into blackness.

Eric felt absurdly lost and out of place and tried to remember the last time he'd changed a tire on a dirt road. At least twenty years, he concluded after a few minutes. Distant sage the color of blue mold surrounded by terra-cotta slabs of exposed rock made him think of Gwen. He still had a postcard she had written when a freshman at Lincoln. All it said was "Colors are my world, Eric."

Not one hundred yards south, an antelope buck stared at him, then ran off. Eric had driven right by him.

Eric restarted the car and drove over a ridge and saw trees. Not just a couple, either, but draws, gullies, and north sides of hills covered with black juniper and pine. Why, all of a sudden, were there trees up ahead? What was different about the soil and climate that trees could grow over there, but not here?

Not for the first time Eric realized he had lost something by learning musical notes but not paying attention to his physical world. He'd dismissed taxonomy as a cold and shallow reference system, a vehicle that never got beyond the comfort of names and classification.

Fall probably knew all the Latin names to these plants, he thought. That's the kind of person he was, always learning and memorizing, categorizing. If he could name it, he could understand it. Eric had begrudgingly admired Ward for his willingness to work—not a common trait among the wealthy. Like Eric taking solace in music, Ward took refuge in ideas. Fall loved Hegel and his systems, a network Eric saw as an exquisitely spoked wheel that went nowhere, a vehicle that, in the end, permitted its inventor to embrace a brutal Prussian regime.

As he crested a hill, he saw a lone cottonwood standing on the left-hand side of the road. A marker on Ward's map. He should turn left at the next driveway. Gravel popped under the pressure of new tires. He went down a long, gentle hill. The prairie on both sides of the road had lost its sagebrush, replaced in some places by lush grass two or three feet tall. In half a mile he saw a battered mailbox with MK RANCH and FALL written on it in large, faded red letters.

A well-used two-track with grass growing between the strips of dirt made up the driveway. Black cows grazed on either side of the road. He drove over two cattle guards, passed two monoliths of neatly stacked hay, then the road curved and dropped into a wide shallow canyon.

Eric saw a wood-sided prefab house and various outbuildings, including a large metal barn, a small older barn drooping on one corner of its foundations, and numerous corrals, all surrounded by hay fields that didn't look like they were getting much water. The valley walls climbed steeply, covered with trees, but broke out into exposed rock and slab at the top.

Eric jammed on the brakes and put the Explorer in park, unable to take in what he saw. He got out and shaded his eyes. Ward Fall couldn't live here. This must be the hired man's house. Ward was a man habituated to certain comforts. Eric had never been to Ward's father's house in Pasadena, but he'd seen the Ladderback and once visited the elegant Nob Hill home of Ward's grandmother. She was the Henniker matriarch. Ward called her Minky.

It was the look in those eyes, those brown scrutinizing eyes of Minky's, that had first sowed the seeds of doubt concerning his friendship with Ward. Despite the original Renoirs hanging on the wall and the butler who met them at the front door, Minky was informal and warm. She paid no attention at all to their hair and patched jeans, but welcomed them as long-awaited guests. The butler brought two ice-cold St. Pauli Girls and chilled glasses on a walnut and silver tray.

Yet she missed nothing. Through a series of seemingly harmless questions, she pegged Eric as an interesting, talented young man who would be part of her grandson's education, but not part of his future. The eyes dictated: *there's an abyss between you and him, one not made for you to breach.*

As Eric got back into the car and eased down the hill, he kept thinking he would see another building: a low, single-story home, built into the hillside, maybe adobe or stucco and with a sweeping redwood deck. The interior would be filled with furniture shipped from San Francisco or Santa Fe. Eric crossed over another cattle guard and found himself in front of the trailer. The road went no farther. He glanced at the odometer. He'd gone thirty-one miles since the last paved road.

Ward said he had to help a neighbor ship cows that day and Lorraine had a town errand and had to meet the boys at the school bus.

Eric parked and got out. The place was tidy and plain; the presence of a single-room weathered log cabin, the sagging wood-shingled barn, and a quartet of venerable apple trees gave evidence someone had settled this land long ago. There was also a tool shed, a chicken coop, two horse trailers, two corrals made of juniper, one smaller corral constructed of rusting steel posts, a very worn early 1970s model Dodge with a wooden flatbed and no license plate, three unidentified pieces of machinery covered in blue plastic, and a yellow John Deere backhoe. There was also a huge well-weeded garden surrounded by an eight-foot fence. The dried corn husks whispered in the wind.

Except for a good view of the Bighorns, Eric felt he could be in a river drainage ranch in the Sand Hills. He smelled rotting compost.

The metal barn looked new, but already had a dent in the side. The prefab was, in fact, a double-wide trailer sided with stained clapboard. It had recently been re-oiled, but that didn't hide the fact it was still a trailer. A flower bed, diligently attended, flanked the walkway, as did two bicycles tipped over on their sides.

The door was unlocked, as Ward said it would be. In fact, Eric noted, the door had no lock at all.

The air smelled of fried meat, an odor so redolent in poorer homes of Valentine. He caught a trace of caraway, a spice he hadn't smelled in years. Fake wooden floors and mass-produced cabinetry with faux veneer greeted him. The living room had a faded red carpet, cheap table and chairs, and a sofa—Eric had to touch it to believe it—covered with a protective plastic cover. Wyoming kitsch.

The two items that gave any indication of an interest in art or music were an ancient oriental rug on the living room floor and a Steinway baby grand. Could it be the same one that had stood upon parquet floors at the Ladderback? It sure looked like it.

He pulled the bench out and opened the keyboard cover and tried to remember what piece he played that afternoon at the Ladderback, the day before Gwen was killed. *Pictures at an Exhibition.* He had taught himself, listening to the record, then broke down and bought the sheet music. Mussorgsky, Eric mused, dead at forty-two, and put into his grave a recognized genius.

He stopped after a couple of chords. The piano was modestly out of tune. He wondered what he was doing in Ward Fall's house. He got up and wandered. There was a room with bunk beds, obviously the haunt of two boys, a small room with a single bed, books, and a collection of bird's nests, a larger bedroom with a queen-sized bed and a sewing machine. Stacks of folded clothing. He glanced into the refrigerator: rows of brown-bottled veterinary medicine lined the shelves on the door. No beer and lots of milk.

He went outside and sat down on the porch and rolled a cigarette, letting the hot sun bake his feet while his face cooled in the shade. Eventually, Eric got up, turned around, and looked at the building. Was the California real estate crash *that* bad? Ward Fall in a trailer. *Incroyable*, as his high school French teacher would exclaim.

Then he turned to the log cabin. It was set on a slope, surrounded by older pines, and probably didn't exceed twenty by twenty. A porch, a recent add-on, provided shade. A look through the window revealed rows of books. Another unlocked door. Books, in fact, lined all four walls. Three spaces had been made for paintings and a rifle cabinet. A small ship's clock ticked away the time. Now this was the Ward Fall Eric remembered. Desk, neat and orderly, sat so that a right-handed person got the benefit of writing with light coming over his left shoulder. CD player. Computer and printer. A hide-a-bed sofa, pulled out and made. Fresh-cut kindling lay in a pile beside the stove.

A wasp buzzed on the windowpane. Eric took out his Leatherman knife and opened it to the scissors. He cut the wasp between the thorax and abdomen. The thorax half writhed on the windowsill.

A dog's toenails clicked on the porch and a black-and-white border collie nudged open the door. The dog barked, then approached Eric, tail wagging tentatively, head lowered in submission, and crouched at his feet. Eric glanced out the window. Ward was astride a horse, bent over, looking in at him through the window, grinning.

"Found the guest quarters already?"

Ward swung down off a sorrel as Eric walked out.

Ward wore a cowboy hat, dirty and sweat-stained plaid shirt, chaps, and dust-covered boots sporting spurs of brass and dull rowels. Eric took in Ward's stature. As a student at Berkeley, he had been a tall, almost skinny kid endowed with the physique found on the basketball court of a small Midwestern college. Now his shirt hung over broad, thick shoulders and muscular chest. A small excuse for a gut protruded over his belt buckle. Eric realized he was sizing Ward up, warrior to warrior, and that his opponent had the complete physical advantage.

Ward's handshake, as it had been in the library, was firm, but he did not seem so nervous. Eric glanced at his clothes again.

"Not exactly the gentleman farmer, Fall."

Ward shook his head. "Very little farming done here except putting in alfalfa and maybe a little spring wheat. Besides, that's an oxymoronic term. A farmer shows no fear of putting his hands in the dirt; a gentleman looks at it and gives instructions on how to put your hands in it."

"Your hideaway?" Eric gestured towards the door of the cabin.

"It's where I run the cow business, such as it is. I come here when the sandman and I have a difference of opinion. During calving I bunk in here so I don't have to come back to bed and wake Lorraine."

Eric thought about the ranch boys he grew up with and how much they hated getting up on March nights to check on calves.

"It gets cold as hell here in the winter, doesn't it?"

"Can. Dry cold, though."

Eric shivered. "Any cold is too cold for me these days. I've gone soft."

Ward looked him up and down like he was appraising a steer. "Need to put some flesh on your frame, Eric. Or is being skin and bones the rage in L.A.?"

Eric took a deep breath. "I don't know, Fall."

He looked around at the rolling sagebrush hills. Heat waves rose on the crests of the barn roof. His eye caught the dent in the metal.

"What happened there? Looks new."

"Yeah," said Ward undoing the throat latch around his horse's neck. "It is new. Both the building and the dent. This spring Josh was pulling the hay wagon loaded with small bales. Tractor lost its brakes. He shut the engine off and jumped just as it hit that building. Wasn't going very fast."

Ward shrugged. "Scared the hell out me, but Lorraine finally got me to see that he did the best he could and no one got hurt. Ranch life. Just like Mattie here." He jerked his head towards the dog. "Got nailed by a rattler last month. I thought she was a goner, but somehow she pulled through."

Eric noted none of the anxiety that had so plagued Ward in the Doe Library.

"So where are we, by the way, Wyoming or Montana?"

"Wyoming. But a twenty-minute walk that way would put you in Montana."

He pointed north. "The ranch is roughly a fifty–fifty split between the states."

"Huh. Mind if I ask: How'd you end up here, Fall?"

Ward nudged his boot on a porch post and shook his head, knowing that no question would be too personal.

"You're implying that choice played a small role in me being here."

"You mean am I deducing or suggesting? Well...." Eric swept

his hand over the landscape as if it were a junkyard, then let his hand collapse at his side.

"Fair question," said Ward, smiling, with apparently no offense taken.

"As you may have heard, my family got into a little financial quagmire. When the dust settled, I had just enough to buy this place."

He looked around and adjusted the reins in his hands. "Great place to raise kids, rattlesnakes excepted. That's probably hard to understand, isn't it? Especially for someone like you who knew me before. Most of my family doesn't understand why I'm here, especially the old man."

"And what does he think?"

Ward laughed. "Caleb Fall? He stayed once for two whole hours, then left. Declared it the most godforsaken piece of real estate he'd ever seen outside of the Yukon and parts of the Sudan. Told me I'd lost my mind."

Ward laughed again, like maybe he was indeed deranged.

"But just about my whole family has said the same thing. My brother enjoys it for the hunting, but wouldn't live here under any circumstances. My sister Susanna liked it for its sparsity and austerity, but she's gone."

"Gone? You mean died?"

"About five years ago. Brain cancer."

"Sorry about that."

"Thanks, well…Minky still visits, though. Remember her?"

"Sure."

"She's ninety-two now and loves it here. She's got bones as fragile as overbaked clay but still comes out every June. She's the only person in the family who understands why I'm here."

"Huh. And it's bigger than Delaware, right?"

"We own a hair less than 20,000 acres, with about a quarter of that being Bureau of Land Management and some state sections."

Eric whistled. "Jesus. Bigger than the Ladderback."

Ward nodded. "Ladderback had better grass, though. Rain

doesn't come down here like it does in the Lost River Range. We only run half the cows on twice that acreage we had in Idaho...."

Ward paused. "I'm going to ask you to watch your epithets. Lorraine takes her religion pretty seriously. It's hard for her to hear what she considers blasphemy."

Eric saw Ward's seriousness and nodded, somehow not surprised. "Sure. How about you, Fall? You got religion, too?"

"I'm trying, I suppose. Lorraine is suspicious of my version. Her faith is pretty tough for a recovering Cartesian."

"What is she?"

"Anabaptist."

"Anabapist? Haven't heard that term in awhile."

"Hutterite. They live in communes. Colonies, as they call they them. Hold everything in common. But, as I believe you know first-hand, communal living can be hard on a body. Lorraine left her colony. She's still pretty serious about her faith, hence the caution on curbing your tongue. Actually, it's just the negative reference to God or Christ that offends her. When annoyed she can let fly with a healthy run of blue."

"Kids still in school?"

Ward looked at his watch. "Lorraine should be returning from the bus stop right about now. Boys have to ride an hour and fifteen minutes each way to school."

He shook his head with regret. "Wish we were closer."

Eric thought of Tavernier. "Every place has a price, Ward. I'll take a long bus ride over a drive-by shooting any day. You wouldn't believe the scum that's risen to the surface in L.A."

Ward looked at him, curious about Eric's vehement tone.

A late-model red Suburban clattered over the cattle guard and bounced down the hill in a cloud of dust. Ward stepped down from the porch and Eric shielded his eyes, curious to see the wife of Ward Fall.

The Suburban stopped and three boys tumbled out, carrying packs and slamming doors. Joshua was unmistakably Ward Fall's son, tall, thin, black hair that flopped around on his head, and serious, intense eyes. The two younger boys, twins, were blond with buzz cuts, didn't look anything like their father. Lorraine walked around the front of the car, somewhat tentative, but not afraid of anything either.

She was short, slightly cherubic, with dirty strawberry blond hair put up in a bun. She wore a calf-length skirt so out of fashion it made Eric's head spin. Reeboks stuck out from under her dress. She had the figure of somewhat slimmed Titian beauty. She approached Ward and Eric and took off her sunglasses. An almost Slavic sweetness, rounded face, and aquamarine eyes greeted Eric. She was, Eric immediately decided, a mere notch above plain, but the presence and acceptance of the world in her step accentuated the good looks she had.

As she reached out to greet Eric, he noticed the ring on her left hand: three stones, including a blueberry-sized ruby accompanied by two diamonds. It was so out of character with the rest of the woman, her plain clothes, her honest face, and her scuffed Reeboks. The ring had obviously come from a Fall family jewelry box, probably his mother's. The larger stone, less valuable from society's point of view, was at the center; the socially prominent stones stood to the side. This was Ward Fall's wife.

She locked eyes with Eric, but then cast them to the side, as if regretting her forwardness. She put out her hand. "I'm Lorraine. Welcome, Eric."

The boys lined up, with Josh stepping up to take Eric's hand. He pumped it like an old friend. The twins offered a perfunctory handshake. One of them said, "Man, Garth Brooks," unable to contain himself.

———

LORRAINE BOWED her head and prayed. "Heavenly Father, we thank you for this meal and company we are fortunate to receive. Thank you for all the blessings you have bestowed upon us today. We ask these blessings in Jesus's name. Amen."

"What kinda grace do you say at your table, Mr. Lindsay?" asked Paul, immediately digging into the beef stroganoff.

"I haven't said grace at a meal for quite a while, Paul."

Paul looked puzzled. "How come?"

"Well, that's okay, none of them Crow say grace either," said Tim.

"Timothy, that's enough," said Lorraine. "And some Crow are Christians."

"That's all right, Lorraine," said Eric, interested to see where the conversation would lead.

But Ward interrupted. "All right, Lindsay, here's the deal. Tomorrow morning we'll get you set up with a horse and bring you up to the rifle range. You can use the .270."

"I brought my own gun."

Ward looked up in surprise. "The hell you say."

"Twenty-five cents, Dad," said Paul solemnly.

"Well, we'll bring 'er out and see what sort of shot you are."

"Sounds like an exam."

"Best prescription against a wounded animal is a good shot. Better get you on a horse, too. When was the last time you rode, Eric?"

"Long time."

"About as long as it's been since you said grace?"

"That's a fair approximation."

"What do you think, boys? Let's put him on Blue Sky."

A circle of impish grins went around the table. Then Tim burst out. "No way, Dad."

Ward laughed and said in a voice carrying a tinge of condescension. "Blue Sky is Lorraine's prospect she bought up on the rez for the grand sum of three hundred dollars. Only mare on the MK. She's a little rough around the edges."

"You have horses, Mr. Lindsay?" asked Timothy.

"Call me Eric. Long time ago I had one."

"What was his name?"

"Her name. Plume."

"You rode mares?" asked Tim.

"Anything wrong with that?" asked Eric, knowing the cowboy's proclivity towards geldings.

"My dad don't like—"

"Doesn't," corrected Ward.

"Doesn't like mares," said the boy. "Says they're too squirrelly. Funny thing is, my friend Justin gots an old mare and she don't—"

"Doesn't," said Ward, again, this time with a bite to his voice.

"Doesn't act like a squirrel."

"Don't be so literal, Timmy. It makes you sound like a dork," said Josh, his faced buried in his plate.

"I am not a dork," said Tim. "Besides, I'm not a letter L."

"Plume could be kind of twitchy," said Eric. "She was half Arab. That's how she got her name. Kept her tail up in the air when she ran. But she was also sweet and could run all day. She required respect, though."

"Like most women I know," said Lorraine.

"Oh, I don't know, hon," said Ward. "I don't think you run with your tail up in the air."

"Oh hush," said Lorraine, smiling.

Timothy pressed on. "What'd she look like? Bet you rode her a lot, huh?"

"Not really. She was kind of light red chestnut. But mostly my sister rode her."

"So where is she now?"

"The horse?"

"Both of 'em."

Ward shifted in his chair.

"Both have died, Tim."

"That's enough questions for now, Timothy," said Lorraine firmly. And this time Eric did not protest her intervention.

AFTER DINNER, Lorraine packed coolers with food. She'd rolled up her sleeves and Eric saw she had arms like a man. Over the last few days she had baked fresh breads and rolls and an apple pie. There were creamy potato soups, sauerkraut, dumplings, and stews. She included a jar of pickled beans. Ward came over and looked at her handiwork. "Put some more stew in this one, Lorraine," or, "We have no need for more than two containers of potatoes."

When Ward was satisfied with the food supply, he and Eric walked to his office. Ward wanted to see Eric's gear. "No need to duplicate anything," he said.

Eric unpacked his bag while Ward inspected his possessions like a quartermaster, sorting the necessary from the unessential, delivering simple pronouncements: "Yes.... No.... Won't work.... Yes.... Don't bring that.... Put it back.... Don't need it.... Already have one."

Eric held up the Filson tin pants and Ward gave a nod of approval. "You bet."

"No pacs?" he asked, then frowned in displeasure when Eric produced his leather boots. "Let's see how they fit. Put them on with one pair of thick socks."

Ward felt all around his foot, having Eric bend that way and this. Finally, he said. "I guess they're okay. They're not the ideal boot for a stirrup. If we get a lot of snow, you're going to have wet feet."

"They're guaranteed waterproof, Fall."

Ward shook his head. "No animal makes a waterproof hide. All leather boots leak eventually, most sooner than the manufacturers like to admit. Have any gaiters?"

"No."

Ward sighed. "That's okay. I'll loan you some."

He turned to the gun case. Eric walked over and undid the locks, opened the lid, and turned the case towards Ward, whose face got very still when he saw what was inside. He picked up the Number One and brought it over to his desk lamp for closer examination.

"When'd you buy this?" he asked after a brief scrutiny.

"Month ago."

"Been shooting it much?"

"Every day."

"What kind of cartridge?"

"One-eighty Nosler."

Ward looked at him curiously then said the first really complimentary thing about his gear. "It's a damned nice rifle. Beautiful piece of walnut," he said almost enviously. "Excellent scope, too. Can't get much better, actually. We'll take it out tomorrow."

Though the window, Eric watched Ward walk back to the house, his hat glowing dully in the moonlight, shoulders starting to droop, but back still erect.

ERIC LAY on the fold-out couch, feeling the frame intrude into his lower back, his head propped up on the pillow that smelled of sweet air. He fouled it with cigarette smoke. The nearly full moon caught traces of the smoke as it rose and flattened in the dark room. So quiet. No traffic, sirens, car alarms, roaring jets, motel room fans, air conditioners, murmur of a freeway, foot traffic in the hall, distant telephones, or even the sound of another person breathing. Even in Redondo there was the sound of the surf. The quiet brought on unease. Eric turned on his cell phone. No service.

Occasionally, wind would blow around a corner of the cabin with enough vigor to raise a low whirr. A coyote yipped in the distance; moments later, the chorus joined in. A metal gate rattled its signature clatter, a sound unmistakable anywhere in the world. Eric eased himself out of bed and looked at the dark rows of books. He turned on the light. The instinct was still there—go read. He'd given up on all books of substance, declaring them a roadblock to building his own system. Yet somehow his own system had never arrived, and the magazines, television, and airplane info fodder superficially satisfied the urge for diversion.

He tried the handle on the twin doors of the gun cabinet. It moved easily. Didn't they lock anything out here? The guns were stored horizontally, like rungs of a lethal ladder. Eric turned on a lamp standing next to the case. There were four rifles with one empty rung on the bottom. He examined each one and noted the rifles were arranged according to caliber: a .220 Swift, a .270 Winchester with a highly worn stock and almost no bluing remaining, a beautifully engraved Mannlicher seven by fifty-seven Mauser, and a Ruger Number One like his, except chambered in .375 H+H magnum. It had iron sights.

Eric examined each rifle, careful not to touch the metal with his bare hands. He surmised the last two guns had come from Caleb Fall's extensive collection. In fact, it surprised him that Ward, who'd apparently lost his fear of firearms, only had four rifles; Ward once told Eric that his father had over one hundred. He noted the absence of a shotgun.

After he replaced the heavy .375 on its rack, Eric noted a leather pouch hanging on the wall of the gun case. It was small, about half the size of his fist, and decorated with some sort of Indian beadwork. It hung in the shadow, dark and undefined. Eric reached to take it off the hook, but suddenly withdrew his hand, filled with a murky feeling that he was intruding. He quickly shut the case and stared at the pouch, now a dusky lump, through the glass. He switched off the light and rolled another cigarette. Standing at the window, he smoked, watching the lights go off in the trailer. He knocked the ashes off his cigarette into his hand, and sang the last bars of "St. James Infirmary" to himself.

————

LORRAINE FRETTED as she performed a whirling choreography between stove and table, simultaneously cooking breakfast and packing lunches.

"You sure you don't want some sausage, Eric? It's made from antelope. Very lean, less than ten percent fat, probably. It's my aunt's recipe. Comes all the way from Russia. Long time ago."

"The sausage or the recipe?"

She smiled broadly, but never took her eyes off the stove.

"A little fruit and coffee's fine, Lorraine, really." He was busy fighting the urge to smoke.

Tim stared at him. "You eat like Minky," he said in a slightly incriminating tone. "She eats nothing but apples and 'naners and oranges for breakfast."

"How do you think she lived to be ninety years old?" said Eric.

"Shoot, I'd be starvin' before I'd get off the dang bus at school," said Paul.

Ward came into the house.

"Man, I love this time of year. Cows shipped early, hay's in, enough standing feed to keep the kine happy for a month. And no snow." He rubbed his hands gleefully then kissed Lorraine. "Time to have fun."

Eric looked at Ward and, for the first time, truly doubted his mission. Where was the low look of desperation he'd seen at Doe? All he'd seen here was a happy, bouncy, lucky bastard with three boys and a devoted wife.

"Easy for you to say," said Tim sullenly, as if picking up on Eric's deliberations. "You get to go elk huntin' and we gots school."

"Tim? What is it with you and your atrocious grammar?" said Ward, sitting down to a plate of food that had more calories than Eric consumed in two days.

"You must have learned that from your mother's backward tongue." He looked at his watch. "Boys, you better be ready to head to the bus stop pronto. Josh, start the Suburban in a minute or two. If we leave on time you can drive."

After Josh left, Eric asked. "How old is he? Twelve?"

"Going on thirteen," said Ward.

"What about the cops?"

Ward snorted. "I haven't perchanced upon a member of the law enforcement establishment on our road for five years, at least."

"I see them every once in a while," said Lorraine, "maybe you don't."

"Yeah, well, I see a game warden or deputy about once a year, but that's about it," said Ward.

Eric found this absence comforting.

Ward worked at putting a thick slab of butter on his toast.

"I thought we'd ride out to the rifle range instead of driving. We can test your saddle and rifle scabbard. While I drive these boys to the bus stop, why don't you go out to the metal corral and acquaint yourself with that flea-bitten gray gelding I tied up next to the gate. His name is Bullet."

"What a reassuring name."

"Isn't it? Don't worry. Bombproof. Packed all three of the boys. The twins ride him together bareback with a rope hackamore. Hoof pick and brush can be found on the shelf left of the tack room door."

Paul motioned to Eric. "C'mon, Mr. Lindsay, I'll show ya."

"Don't tarry, Paul. The school would suffer mightily without you."

"Sure, Dad."

TWO-HUNDRED-DOLLAR Olathe cowboy boots sank into spongy dried cowshit.

Ward came back from the school bus run and walked towards the barn with a determined gait, like a child half-running out the schoolhouse door on a Friday afternoon. Then he slowed and eventually stopped short of the tack room door. He stared at the ground for a long time. Eric watched him, deliberately brushing the broad expanse of Bullet's back. Ward turned, looking somber. "How do you feel about killing animals?"

Eric shrugged, wondering what was going through Ward's head. "Little late for such philosophical queries, don't you think?"

"Perhaps, but I don't care for it myself."

"Why are we hunting?" he had to ask.

Ward nodded and gave Eric a knowing look, but said slowly, "A worthy question deserving a solid answer. I guess on the basest level I like elk meat. I like the hunt. It's the shooting I get less enthralled with each year."

"Then why don't you try camping without guns?"

"Tried that one year. My brother and I fished. Wasn't the same.

Then it got cold. Had a hell of time getting that fly through two inches of ice. The query of the moment is, however: do you feel like hunting?"

This is not part of the game plan, thought Eric.

"No guarantee I'll shoot something," Eric said casually.

"Fair enough," said Ward and turned back into the tack shed.

He came out carrying a saddle in one hand and pad in the other. With ease and confidence he set them on his horse. The man could do it in his sleep.

They saddled up Bullet together and Eric swung onto the horse.

"How's that feel?"

"Tolerable. So far." Ward came around and adjusted the length of the stirrup by one hole.

"We'll keep 'er at a walk."

On the trip to the rifle range, Eric renewed his distrust of riding and horses. He was cold and his ass ached within fifteen minutes of being mounted on Bullet's broad back. The horse seemed only nominally interested in obeying his commands, but not in a panic to do anything dangerous, either.

They rode along a path next to a fence, then turned onto a two-track that wandered through scraggly copses of ponderosa. They came to a meadow growing back to forest and followed the road to a gravel pit where they dismounted and tied up the horses.

Using a bulldozer, Ward had made a rifle range with a mound of gravel as the backstop. A crude but sturdy spiked-together table of rough sawn lumber made up a shooting bench. He saw that Ward had anticipated their visit and tacked up a series of targets. Hitting the 100-yard target, clear and bright orange in the scope's cross-hairs, seemed effortless. On his fifth and final shot, he imagined Ward's close-clipped head at the bull's eye and pulled the trigger. The gun seemed to go off by itself.

Ward's eyebrows raised when they walked to the bank of gravel and examined the target. His put his fingers to the bullet holes, measuring them with his knuckle.

"Five shots under an inch at 100 yards. Two overlapping holes. Hard to beat that group. "

"It's the rifle."

"Unlikely," said Ward, who walked back to the bench and took up the .270.

He rested it on the wood then searched his coat pocket for shells. "I better run a few rounds through this rifle just to be sure. Josh and some of his friends were using it prairie dog hunting last month. Somebody might have slammed the scope in the door."

Ward held up the gun, rubbing the scarred fore-end. "Looks like hell, doesn't it? I've considered cleaning it up, but given its origins, I decided I best leave it as it is. I changed the scope and mounts, that's all."

He jacked a shell into the chamber and flipped the safety off. "A pre-64 Winchester. Came from a very unlikely source," he said.

He shot once, ejected the shell, caught it midair, then jacked in another round.

He peeped through the scope.

"Off to the left a hair. A Crow. He'd been stealing a cow from me each year since I bought the place. Burned my ass at first then I just chalked it up to the cost for doing business next to the reservation. A few years ago he developed amyotrophic lateral sclerosis. Apparently he wanted to set matters right before he entered the spirit world."

Ward fired again and looked into the scope.

"That's better. One more. His wife or girlfriend, I don't know who she was, really, drove him to our house. Lorraine was alone when he came. The twins weren't even two years old. She told me she started praying when she saw an Indian walk unsteadily up to the house with a rifle in hand."

Eric felt transfixed by the words, not quite believing them.

"Jesus."

Ward continued. "Yeah. That's what I thought, too. Then she just accepted whatever was going to happen was God's will. But this

Crow just gave her the rifle, mumbling. Took me a month of asking around the rez before I figured out the story."

"Lorraine didn't try to hide herself or the kids? She just accepted this Indian might have been Death strolling up the walk?"

"She's a notoriously poor judge of people. She believes everyone is good."

Eric tried to imagine what it would be like to live such fatalism. Ward pulled the trigger the third time; the report made Eric jump.

———

SIZE SEVEN blue jeans flapped in the wind, an empty field behind them. Lorraine sang loudly and obviously for her own pleasure. She had a strong voice, sure of itself and laced with a little vibrato. Eric recognized the song, "His Eye Is on the Sparrow," an old gospel number based on verses from the Book of Matthew. She was on key.

Let not your heart be troubled. His tender word I hear
And resting on His goodness, I lose my doubts and fears;
Though by the path He leadeth, but one step I may see;
His eye is on the sparrow, and I know He watches me;
His eye is on the sparrow, and I know He watches me.

Lorraine hung the last pair of pants on the line, picked up the laundry basket, then stopped when she noticed Ward and Eric riding through the gate. She smiled and waved enthusiastically then went back into the house. There was some of Gwen in that woman: her earnestness, her seriousness. Not necessarily the same curiosity, however.

They stripped the horses of their tack and tied them up to the trailer. Ward disappeared into the trailer tack room, rearranging various items. "Let's start loading," he said, his voice booming.

Lorraine had set all their gear in a pile on the porch. Ward checked it carefully, as if doubting Lorraine's capacity to be thorough. He bent down and picked up a cooler and turned to Eric. "Stick this against the far wall of the trailer's tack room."

Eric took the cooler. As he walked away he suddenly felt dizzy. He slowed his pace, the cooler banging on his thighs. By the time he reached the tack room, nausea had set in. He set the cooler down and knelt on the rubber floor, his elbows resting on the top of the cooler. He did not want Ward to catch him in this state. That could foul up plans. Then the nausea subsided as quickly as it came. Ward walked around the trailer. Eric stood and from the tack room window saw Lorraine come out of the house drying her hands on her apron.

"Ward? Telephone. It's Andy Wistrom from the auction barn. I told him you were busy but he says it's important."

Ward set his load down on the tack room floor, not even looking, and grumbled softly, "Hell," his voice barely audible. "Importance is but a point of view."

Ward walked to the house and disappeared with Lorraine following. Eric stepped out of the tack room, feeling better. This was not the first time he'd felt such a sensation.

As he turned up the walk for another load, Ward emerged from the house in intense conversation with Lorraine. Eric stopped, watching. Lorraine swung towards the door, her hand hung on the frame. She shook her head as if that was the last word and went into the house. Ward walked back to the trailer, the wind obviously taken from his sails. Something was amiss.

Ward threw up his hands in mock helplessness. "Well, best laid plans, eh pilgrim? It appears the 4V will sell five hundred sync-bred cows at auction. Today. Three o'clock."

He took off his hat.

"Shit," he said soberly. "No prior notice or anything. I've been coveting that herd for years. The Towson family has been teetering on the financial brink for some time now. Made them plenty of offers. All I got were stall tactics. Too proud. Now Andy tells me the old man called him up an hour ago and told him to make room for five hundred cows at today's auction. That's everything. The whole herd. Man, he must be desperate. That's the only reason he'd ever sell without giving notice."

He put his hat back on. "Better go, Eric," he said with genuine regret. "I tried to get Lorraine to go buy them for us, but it's a dispersal sale. She feels to buy cows under such conditions abets poverty and is nothing short of arrant opportunism. Logical discussions to the contrary prevail nothing with that woman. God damn. Sometimes her backwardness exasperates me."

Then Ward turned away, just as he had turned away when Eric had asked about the Ladderback. He said quietly and wearily, the anger out of his voice: "And she knows more about a cow than I do. Well, it's going to delay us a day. I won't get back until late tonight."

"See?" said Eric, feeling anxious. "Didn't I tell you we'd spend time at cow auctions during my vacation?"

Ward shook his head. "I get disagreeable at auctions. Ask Lorraine. Dislike the whole process, actually. Leaves too much to chance. I guarantee that when the word gets out that Towson's Black Angus are going on the block, half the cattlemen in eastern Montana are going do just what I am about to do: drop what they're doing and head for the auction house and spend money they don't have. I'll be churlish coming and going."

Eric felt a pang of exclusion and feared his plan might be thwarted.

"In fact," Ward said, "it might be good time for you and Lorraine to get better acquainted."

Eric didn't like that idea.

"She doesn't have time for entertaining guests, does she?"

"She'll make time. She might even put you to work."

"All right," Eric said, seeing that Ward's mind was made up. Don't push anything, he said to himself.

"Good," Ward said, palpably relieved. "Now let's untie the horses from the trailer and turn them out in the corral. Take those coolers out of the trailer, too."

After unhooking the trailer, Ward left, carrying a notebook and the ranch checkbook in his right hand, his mind obviously on the sale. The wrinkles on his face looked more pronounced than ever.

Eric and Lorraine brought the coolers back in from the porch. She unpacked them and returned material to the refrigerator and freezer. When she was done, she stood erect and sighed. "There. Coffee?"

"Sure."

She poured the beans into the grinder, then deliberately took one or two beans out and threw them back in the coffee bag.

"Afraid it's going to be too strong?"

Lorraine looked up, embarrassed at having to explain her actions. "Oh, no. It's just..." she paused, then straightened up, as if to make a stand. "I always put a few beans back every time I make coffee. It reminds me that I can be happy with less. It's human to want too much."

She smiled in a dreamy sort of way. "I always think of Ward when I make coffee."

"How so?"

"I was at a cattle sale in Billings. It was cold, really cold, and the heater at the barn wasn't working worth a darn. I wasn't paying attention to who was sitting next to me, but all of a sudden I smelled this really delicious coffee odor. I looked around and saw the man next to me was pouring coffee from a thermos."

The kettle came to a boil.

She relaxed a little, but remained at the counter, the top to the coffee grinder in her hand.

"The smell reminded me of the strong coffee I used to drink at my mother's colony up in Alberta. Ward looked right at me and handed me the cup."

She turned away, still smilingly, blushing at the memory.

"I loved the fact that he, a complete stranger, offered me a sip from his cup, like he'd known me all along."

"And...?"

She smiled openly, almost as a child would. "I drank. It was black and bitter. I was in trouble and I knew it."

"So what was a Hutterite woman doing buying cows?"

She took the kettle off the stove.

"My dad was herd boss for the colony, but he had to go to a meeting somewhere. The herd boss apprentice was sick that day. Everybody knew that I drove a mean bargain. Hutterite women aren't really supposed to do that sort of work, but like everywhere else, when you really want to get the job done, have a woman do it," she said with a wry smile.

"Except dispersals?" said Eric.

"No. No dispersals," she said with finality. She poured the water into the coffee press. "One of the saddest things you'll ever see is a family farm or ranch going under. Don't want any part of it. My father wouldn't attend dispersals either. Ward thinks I'm crazy."

She opened a window. "The sun can heat up this mobile home. Better have some circulation."

Outside the breeze bent the seedless heads of the grass and thistle. Lorraine stood still, soaking up the sight. "It's beautiful, isn't it? Every day I think: 'This is beautiful.' I wonder if I'll ever get tired of it."

She turned. "I doubt it."

She stood before the press, waiting. The more Eric looked at her, the more he felt agitation growing within him. He hadn't counted on being alone in a home with Ward Fall's wife.

"Ward taught me to make coffee like this. At first I thought he was just being a weird picky food guy, but I changed my mind."

She looked out the window again.

"Ward says you're a really talented musician."

Eric looked down at the counter not knowing where to go with the conversation. Maybe he better slip away to Ward's office.

"I get by."

"You must do more than that. Written any songs?"

"A few."

She plunged down the press and poured. "Cream or sugar? Could you play me one?"

"Black. Sorry. I need my guitar for that."

She handed a cup to Eric. "Something tells me, Mr. Lindsay, that you play the piano just fine."

He remembered her singing while hanging laundry.

"Okay. I'll play one of my songs if you sing one of yours."

"Mine?"

"A favorite."

"One from my church, maybe?"

"Sure. Whatever. That would be fine."

She bowed her head, embarrassed, her hand halfway over her mouth.

In the living room he sat down on the piano bench and opened the lid. He played a few chords, then his hands began the opening measures of "That's Love Walking Out the Door."

Lorraine interrupted. "Wait a minute, mister. I want an original song."

"You recognize that song?" He silently exhaled in mild exasperation, wanting to get through this process as quickly as possible.

"Billy Madden," Lorraine said. "It was a hit."

"Yes, it was, and I wrote it."

"You did? How come it has his name on it?" Look. She walked across the room and pulled a Madden CD off the shelf. "See?"

"Did Ward buy that?" he asked.

"No, I did. He has such a nice voice."

"Grade-A tenor. Billy had a smash first release. A million-selling CD. Then he dried up. Happens all the time. Couldn't write those hit songs anymore. Or at least he couldn't write them as fast as his recording contract stipulated that he do. He got a very lucrative contract after that first release, but it came with conditions. One of them was he had to record original material. He ran out of time. That's when I entered the picture. I had a couple songs lying around I thought he might like. He gave them a listen and we cut a deal, just like you and I cut a deal. He took my songs and paid me."

Lorraine looked confused. "Then it should be your name below this song."

"Not when you sell the rights and the title. In the music business it's called 'collaboration.' But I did write that song, that and two others on that CD, as a matter of fact. 'Emilene,' and what is the other one? 'Road to Nogales.' Isn't that on there?"

"Yes, it is. My kids like that one. You write the lyrics, too?"

"Lyrics, too."

"That's true humility, giving up your name like that," she said staring at the CD cover.

"Were it so noble, Lorraine. It paid the bills for a few years, then that too went to hell."

"Funny," said Lorraine, still looking a little addled. "You don't strike me as country western type of person."

"Oh? And what type of person do I strike you as?"

"Jazz, maybe. I don't know. You and that ponytail. But I've never been around many musicians. What made you to write that song?"

Wanting to turn the conversation around, he declined to give the details. "Well, you want to hear the rest of the song?"

"Yes. You've got to sing it, too." Her eyes watched his hands on the keyboard as he slowly moved through the chords.

"You don't know what kind of caterwauling you're asking for."

"What? Ward said you had a good voice."

"I can carry a melody and harmonize to a limited degree, that's all. No range. What else did Ward tell you about me?"

He stopped playing. Lorraine looked at the floor, then back at him.

"He said…" She hesitated "He said he had never met anybody before with such an array of God-given talents."

"Funny. I would have said the same thing about Ward."

"But," she continued, "he said you were the recipient of many unopened gifts."

Eric laughed. "Now that's charitable."

He picked up the tempo and began singing, pleased that he could remember the words. When he finished, she applauded, clapping her hands enthusiastically.

"Now it's your turn," he said.

"Well, all right. You accompany me?"

"Sure."

She took a book from off the top of the piano and flipped through it. "Okay. Let's try this one. It's kinda old, really."

Eric glanced at the song then out the window at the backyard at a small pasture of uncut hay. Sun reflected off the telephone wires. He did not need the sheet music to play "Leaning on the Everlasting Arms." He'd played the same tune for his Aunt Ula, thirty years before, also overlooking a hayfield.

An unadorned voice, concentrated and strong as Sicilian olive oil, came out of Lorraine's mouth. She knew the words by heart. She closed her eyes and sang like she was performing before an audience who loved her and would accept any mistake she might make. Her breasts rose and fell, right hand moving back and forth, conducting herself. Where had she taken lessons? he wondered. No. She wouldn't. That would be vanity. She sang with self-taught conviction, a solidity no conservatory could instill. It thrilled him and simultaneously evoked an uncomfortable feeling in his spine, a feeling that all humans get when they hear or see something truly authentic.

He had heard this type of voice before in Nashville. Girls coming out of the Ozarks or the hollows of Kentucky. Mountain canaries, they called them. To a soul, the country western machine ravaged them, sucking their energy and spirit dry with arachnid vigor, sending them back to dirt roads or careers as waitresses.

What a fellowship, what a joy divine,
leaning on the everlasting arms;
What a blessedness, what a peace is mine,

leaning on the everlasting arms.
Leaning, leaning, safe and secure from all alarms;
leaning, leaning, leaning on the everlasting arms.
Oh how sweet to walk in this pilgrim way,
leaning on the everlasting arms;
Oh how bright the path grows from day to day,
leaning on the everlasting arms.
What have I to dread, what have I to fear,
leaning on the everlasting arms?
I have blessed peace with my Lord so near,
leaning on the everlasting arms.

At the end of the last line, she opened her eyes, and sank a little in stature, beads of perspiration on her upper lip and face flushed, and looked a little embarrassed. She cocked her head like a chicken as if to reestablish her demeanor. She touched her hair wrapped around the top of her head. It must be long, Eric thought to himself. Lorraine looked at him and saw that he was staring right at her. He dropped his eyes to the keyboard.

"You're not saved yet, are you?" She asked the question with the same tone a desirous woman might ask a committed man: *You're married, aren't you?*

"No."

"It's never too late."

"That's what my Aunt Ula used to say to my mother: 'Never too late.'"

Lorraine nodded. "She was saved?"

"My mother? If ever there was a case for eternal damnation she is it. But Ula, yes. She was my mother's younger sister. She left Valentine pretty young, right after high school, I think, and ended up outside Wichita. She converted to Pentacostalism and came to visit once a year. I saw her in rapture once, Bible in hand, sitting on the top step of our back porch with Gwen in Valentine. Scared me. And yet it filled me with a sense of wonder. My father came up from behind and put his arms around us, told us not to be frightened, told us it was just another form of music. Music from above. That's what he called it, understandable only by those who could read holy notes."

Lorraine again nodded her head.

"What about Ward? You got him to convert?"

"Still working on him. I knew when we married it would be a struggle. The colony was dead set against it, of course, but by that time I wasn't spending much time there. Hardly any at all."

She stopped talking and turned again to the window, twisting her wedding ring around like a loose pipe fitting.

"Eric, you don't know how Ward suffers. Nightmares." She stopped. "It happened this spring, but usually it happens in July, when it gets hot for the first time all season. And then we have a rain, usually when our first cutting is lying on the ground, it seems. For just a day we have humidity here. When that happens, Ward gets so down. It hangs on him for weeks. The weather reminds him of the day of the accident. He goes days without saying anything. Can't sleep, sometimes for weeks. He's been hospitalized twice since we've been married."

Lorraine stepped beside the piano bench and took Eric's right hand. She placed it on the keyboard, her own hand on top of his. Eric could feel the dampness in her palm.

"These fingers are on the keyboard only for a while. Do you understand? Just as this is temporary," she pulled back the curtain and pointed to the landscape. "Please, won't you please speak to Ward while you're here? I know it must be hard for you, too. Your sister's in heaven. I know. She's in a good place."

"I don't know if my sister met your qualifications for entrance into heaven."

She nodded. "The death of an innocent has an unexpected path."

"That sounds like something Ward would say."

"No," she said. "Those are my words. Ward's would be more complicated."

She took her hand away.

He let his hand go flat on the keyboard, depressing no notes, then excused himself to go smoke outside, leaving his coffee untouched.

IT WAS long past dark by the time Ward turned off the Interstate. The auction had lasted twice as long as he anticipated, but it had been well worth the trip. He'd bought over eighty cows. Luckily for him, another dispersal at an auction house in Miles City pulled away potential buyers in Billings. The good deal would worry Lorraine, who was always concerned that a bargain wasn't good for someone else.

They'd lost a day of hunting, which he regretted. Lorraine simply would not go to the auction for him. She had considered his request for several seconds then shaken her head, smiled with her lips pressed tightly together, and said sorry. She suggested that he and Eric drive to Billings, attend the auction, then continue on to elk camp. The idea didn't sit well with him and, in the end, he was grateful he hadn't taken her advice. Towson's cattle arrived late. They would have been forced to drive up the mountain in the dark. Not an implausible scenario, one he'd done before, but didn't feel like doing with Eric Lindsay.

There was no direct route to Hake's Fork. Once you turned off the Interstate it was just mile after mile of marginal road on the Crow and Cheyenne reservations. A bad experience had visited him on these roads a year ago as he drove back alone from looking at a colt in Hardin. It had snowed that morning, cleared, and briefly warmed up. But the pavement went slick the minute the December sun dropped below the horizon. He came around a curve to see fresh car tracks veering off the road into the snow. He stopped and got out. He heard the whining of wheels getting nowhere. In the rapidly gathering dark, he saw a rusted yellow Chevy Blazer, rear wheels spinning like fury, trying to back out of the burrow ditch.

The Blazer's front bumper was against the fence; its four-wheel-drive either wasn't engaged or wasn't working. An Indian sat cursing behind the wheel. He stopped when he saw Ward and grinned. Ward skidded down the bank and went to the car window. The driver, a Cheyenne, Ward thought by his almost Asian features, was very drunk, but not as far gone as the woman next to him. She was passed out.

Ward hesitated. This was tricky business. If he pulled them out, a slick road with marginal visibility would be made even more dangerous by a drunk driver. If he left them here, they could freeze. The temperature was already in the low twenties and was forecast to drop to the single digits. Better just offer them a ride to Lame Deer.

But the man wouldn't hear of it and became irritated at the suggestion of a ride. "You trying to tell me I can't drive, man?" he asked.

Ward let the notion drop and went to get his tow line and gloves. The Indian got out the car and stood by the rear bumper. When Ward returned and bent down to attach the hook to the bumper, the man struck him hard at the base of the neck.

Ward saw dots of light and went down, face in the snow. The Indian was on him, striking him and shouting, over and over. *"Give me the keys, give me the fucking keys to your truck!"*

Ward didn't have the keys; they were in the ignition. The truck had never been turned off. The man was heavy but slow and drunk. Ward flipped him over and got up, his head and neck throbbing. He ran up the embankment, the Indian in pursuit, too inebriated give much of a chase but still shouting about the keys. Ward barely had time to unhook his tow rope before the Indian caught up with him, grabbing at his pant leg with a crashing fall. Ward kicked him off, his heel smashing the Indian in the lip, and jumped in his truck. He took off, peering into his rear view mirror at the Indian lying in the road, his head down. Ward felt as if he'd lost a lot more than just a tow rope.

Now, as he approached the spot of the incident, he slowed, as if he expected to still see the Blazer and the man lying on the road. They were gone, of course, but suddenly, in front of the headlights appeared the shape of an enormous black bull. Ward put on the brakes and the bull turned towards the truck with baleful eyes.

Now where in the hell had this guy come from? Who owned him? There wasn't a gate around for at least a couple miles each way. Both sides of the road were fenced. Ward tried to think if anyone he knew leased this tribal land. Was it just being grazed by a Cheyenne? He looked for a brand or ear tag and could see none. He had a slightly curly coat.

This wasn't any ordinary animal. It was probably the largest Angus that Ward had ever seen: long, flat back with a huge hump at the base of his neck. Must weigh 2,500 pounds and sire one big calf, he thought. I'm not sure I'd want a calf that big, though. Birthing nightmare. The bull heaved a snort and bedded down, blocking the road. The cab was suddenly filled with the sharp acrid smell of burning garbage. Ward opened the door to shoo him off the road when he suddenly felt fearful and thought better of his plan.

He sat there, the diesel idling, lights spotting the bull, and his heart pounding, not knowing what to do. He hoped somebody would come along so they, whoever the driver was, could help him move this beast. But no lights arrived. So he put the truck in four-wheel drive and skirted the animal, whose eyes followed him as he passed, driving on the steep bank of the road.

Ward felt shaken and a dark foreboding overtook him, one he dreaded, and within five miles of passing the bull he felt himself slide into a black fog. By its speed and power, he knew the spell was going to be a bad one. All he could think was: *For Jesus's sake why did I let Lorraine talk me into having Lindsay here?* Ward was surprised that he'd been able to spend even a day with him and not feel low. He'd had a bad black spell after coming back from the reunion last spring. Pulling out required heavy doses of medication.

His thoughts turned to what could help alleviate his blackness. Usually he counted on daily feeding to help him out, especially during winter's short days, a time when he was vulnerable to dark tides. He loved this activity more than any other on the ranch. Ward would not have any truck with round bales, those convenient two-ton bundles of hay and alfalfa that could be rolled out each morning like unraveling a cinnamon bun. Instead, he continued to use small, rectangular bales that required stacking, unstacking, and feeding, flake by flake, to his stock.

Those mornings at thirty below zero beckoned him out of bed quicker than warm days of summer. He wanted to be in the presence of animals that could withstand such cold. Inside the trailer, the propane furnace would roar all night, clanking and huffing, attempting to meet the thermostat's demands. The walls and roof contracted and expanded. The nails popped in the redwood siding. Cottonwood logs in the stove burned with fury, then sank into a bed of snapping coals.

But beneath an open sky, it was still on these mornings, all but for the cock pheasant off in the hawthorn, who tutted in disapproval of the cold. His haystacks always looked smaller in winter, as if they'd suddenly shrunk along with the drop in temperature. When the cold came, Ward partook in the ancient worry of any rancher in northern climates—did he have enough feed? In October, his two stacks were monoliths of well-cured green timothy and brome, talismans against winter. By January they looked positively puny.

He fed the horses first. In order to conserve energy, they stood as still as their terra cotta brethren unearthed from a Qin tomb. White shards of hoarfrost hung on their lashes. On one particularly cold day last winter, he'd found the nasal passages of Blue Sky all but blocked from condensed breath. After snowstorms, a two-inch layer of snow would sit on their backs for days, the sign of healthy, heavy coats. Sometimes afternoon sun would partially melt the snow; then it would refreeze at dusk and produce a row of icicles hanging from their bellies. The horses looked like they belonged on a carrousel from a Nordic fairy tale.

When he arrived with hay, their shoeless hooves squeaked on the dry snow as they shifted their weight. Slowly, they walked over to the fence, ears pricked forward. When Ward cut the strings and scattered the flakes of hay, he was greeted by a rush of summer: the tang of cured alfalfa, the faded green of brome, seedheads still intact, the purple heads of orchard grass. He scattered the flakes so Bullet, the alpha horse, wouldn't hog it all.

Driving to feed the cattle he felt gratitude for the heated cab of his tractor. He loved to see his young bulls bedded down under the box elder after a snowstorm, north flanks covered with snow, south sides, black and bare.

Beneath the maelstrom of depression, he remained convinced that practicing a simple way of life would sponsor an elemental state of mind. This didn't mean that life would be uncomplicated, but a routine, day after day, of simple tasks would tame the part of his brain that dictated that life had to be sophisticated and complex in order to be fulfilling. His eldest sister, Susanna, an ordained Buddhist nun when she died, and Lorraine of course, had taught him this.

His brother Fredrick's life, and those of his cousins, were enormously complicated, and Ward felt appreciative to be happy with simplicity. With every slab of hay he tossed off the wagon, he gave in to the universe. *Give in. Give in.* He often found himself saying it out loud some mornings, although he had no idea what he was giving in to.

At night, to stave off cravings for whiskey—which only gave temporary relief, then provided fuel for a very steep and rapid descent—he'd retreat to his study and listen to the last movement of Mahler's *Resurrection* Symphony so loud it made the face of his ship's clock rattle. But he knew that on this night Eric was in his study, asleep or counting the bullets for his .308.

CHAPTER 5

THE SILHOUETTE OF WARD'S HEAD, already in a cowboy hat, poked through the door. "Hit the deck, city boy. Time to head to the high country."

Eric turned on the light and looked at his watch: 4:55.

When Eric got beyond the porch light's glare, he saw the dim shapes of horses tied to the trailer. Two people at work. Josh and Ward. When Eric reached the trailer, Ward peered over Bullet's neck and said in his best info-tone. "We're done. You can go in the house."

Timothy and Paul sat quietly at the breakfast table sipping hot chocolate, their eyes swollen with sleep. Lorraine, working at a counter, glanced over her shoulder. "Morning, Eric. Sleep well?"

She was trying to sound cheerful, but seemed flustered.

"Not bad," he lied.

"Coffee?"

"Please." He looked at the twins.

"How come you guys are up so early?"

"Dad got us up," said Timothy, looking into his mug. "He said Mom needs to cook just one breakfast in the morning."

Lorraine, face registering strain, brought the coffee over. Ward came in quiet and gray, his exuberance of yesterday gone. Josh followed. Ward's eyes carried defeat; Eric breathed an audible sigh of relief. Ward sat down, elbows on the table, and waited for his food, looking blankly in front of him, the way a deep-sea diver might before descending to a newly sunken ship where bloated faces waited behind portholes.

Ward put his head down and only the utensils talked. Lorraine served scrambled eggs with chopped ham. The children were subdued before their plates, clearly afraid of puncturing an uneasy calm. When Ward finished eating he handed his plate to Lorraine and jerked his head towards Eric. "C'mon," he said, sighing, and pushed back his chair.

Ward stood behind the twins and placed a large hand on each of their necks, rubbing them gently like they were worry beads. He bent over and lightly kissed the tops of their heads. "Mind your Mom," he said, then turned towards the door, putting his hand on Josh's left shoulder, letting it stay there momentarily.

Lorraine followed them, as did Josh. At the foot of the porch steps she put her hands out to touch Ward's coat. He stopped, almost reluctantly, and turned. Lorraine put her arms around him and her head on his chest, hugging him. He hugged her back; momentarily they became one lump. In the bluish light of dawn Eric saw her lips silently move and realized she was praying. He turned away. Tim and Paul looked stonily out the window, then Paul offered a timid wave.

The sun had edged over a butte by the time they pulled out of the ranch road and headed north. Eric noticed the SURRENDER IS NOT SLAVERY message on the dash, but said nothing.

They drove along washboard roads, the box elder and cottonwood brilliant in the creek bottoms, yellow and roaring red fireworks against a blue sky. Cows wandered among the sagebrush and river-bottom alfalfa fields still green. Pine covered the hills, with south facing slopes bearing runty specimens. The truck, the diesel humming and thrumming, climbed and up and down hills, into and out of sunlight, past Indian housing, each with a satellite dish, no matter the trash outside. The roads got better and better the farther they got from Hake's Fork.

Eventually valleys gave way to rolling hills with more black cows and only the occasional cottonwood or butte. Oddly, the closer they came to the mountains, the flatter and more fertile the fields became. Some were already being tended for winter fallow, plowed and harrowed arrow straight. But for the mountains that stood before them, the county almost had a Nebraska feel. Then, within the stretch of a few miles, the fertility disappeared; nothing but short grass, eroded draws, sagebrush, overgrazed pasture, and bales of hay, left out in the field and half eaten. Up ahead, blue and cold, were the Bighorns and to the north, the Pryors.

At a nondescript paved road littered with potholes, Ward turned left, then took his foot off the accelerator as they approached a boxy ranch house with two dogs who watched the truck drive by. Ward pointed to the house and said, "That's where my friend Tommy Yellow Legs lives." His voice had a mortician's flatness. It was the first time he'd spoken in a hundred miles.

"Once the meanest drunk in southern Montana. Crazy drunk. Scared the shit out of everyone, including me. Before he dried out I watched him intimidate six cops outside the Jim Town bar. I recall wondering what in the hell a Crow was doing outside a bar filled with Northern Cheyenne. But such is the power of Tommy. Big medicine. A hunter and tracker of the first order. He can read the ground like scripture. Does forensic work for the BIA and the Montana State Police. If there's a suspicious death on the rez, especially in the middle of nowhere, he's the first person they send to the scene."

Eric took in this information, relegating it to a recess deep in his brain. He would ponder the ramifications later. Right now he had a job to do.

Past Yellow Legs's house, the road went to dirt. Ruts, heaves, and crude water bars appeared. Ward knocked the truck into four-wheel drive and kept glancing back at the trailer, using the rear view mirror. They crested a saddle and suddenly the foothills gave way to the north flank of the Bighorns. Between talus slides, tongues of dark fir and aspen turning gold jutted down like mottled syrup sliding off a steep-sided pastry. Then came smooth meadows, somehow spared erosion, that blasted the eye with brilliant bursts of ochre dried grass. The color reminded Eric of a blond-topped Gibson Hummingbird he once owned.

"The wind is blowing," said Ward. "Look at that antenna. That's both good and bad for elk hunting, mostly good. Can't hear us in the woods." That info-tone again. Flat. No emotion. No footnotes.

Then came another one. "We're off the reservation now."

The road began following a creek. Shadows crossed the dashboard and they were in a shallow ravine, brilliant red chokecherry and withered hawthorn lining the road. The truck and trailer rattled across a bridge and strained into a steep hairpin turn. They sidehilled up the mountain, passing through a patchwork of landscapes: thin soil, exposed rock, and overgrazed gullies, then up a very steep stretch kept cool by older pine and spruce. The sun glared when they emerged from these sylvan tunnels; Eric squinted as they rumbled into the heat of old clear cuts and burns with gray stumps. They went through a section recently blackened by fire. The ground beneath these trees was charred, broken only by chalky rock and a desolate blanket of rust-colored needles. The road finally flattened out, and they drove for what seemed an eternity, the sun baking overhead. Along a ridge of chalk white cliffs, the road forked, and Ward took the one marked with a sign: DEAD END 12 MILES.

Occasionally the truck passed another wall tent or parked truck with a camper on the back. The road got rougher. Ward put the truck into second gear and left it there. Finally they got to a metal gate posted with a bullet-riddled yellow Forest Service sign that read PRIVATE LAND BEYOND THIS GATE. Then a faded sign with stenciled letters: KOBCZYNSKY LAND AND CATTLE COMPANY. NO TRESPASSING.

They got out to unlock the gate.

"In an otherwise ill-fated life, getting this cow camp was Stanley Kobczynsky's greatest piece of luck," Ward said as he fiddled with the lock.

"Who's he?"

"He's the K in MK. Polish immigrant who saved his money digging coal and started the ranch. Bought a bunch of abandoned homesteads and put them into one piece. Had four sons and World War One took every one. His wife succumbed to the influenza epidemic."

Ward shook his head as if the sorrow derived from this list of declaratives was his. "But sometime during the nineteen-twenties, or so the story goes, Stan won this place in a card game. Took it away from a prominent Sheridan landowner. It's a half section, a chunk of ground surrounded on all four sides by national forest. Got a spring, corrals, and a cabin."

"And who's the M?"

"McConnell. Fitz John McConnell. A land-crazed Irishman who apparently first patented the original homestead."

Eric thought some of his cheer might be coming back, but after this professorial outburst Ward shut down.

Low-slung, with a sagging porch and a shingled roof supported by a weary ridge line, the log cabin faced southeast with its back tucked against the hillside. Two rusting pieces of stovepipe poked out at opposite ends of the roof. In contrast to this decrepitude, new concrete glared out from the under the dark logs.

Ward saw him inspecting the foundation. "Had to pour new footings last year. Don't you know it was a bitch getting a concrete truck in here. Driver got stuck on the way in. I'm here to testify that getting a stuck, loaded, concrete truck unstuck constitutes a serious proposition."

Then his voice trailed off and he unlocked the door.

Two rooms, smelling of must and damp wood, divided the cabin: sleeping quarters and a kitchen/eating area, with a stove in each room. The sleeping room had two sets of bunk beds against the north wall and two double beds. The rooms were dark.

Ward flopped his bedroll down on one of the beds. "Take your pick. Let's take the plywood off the windows. After we unload, prime the pump with the water in the bucket beside the kitchen stove. Pump it for a good three minutes until you get clear, cold water."

Eric tested the rest of the beds and chose the least boggy mattress on a bottom bunk. He checked his tobacco supply and went out the back door, up a creaking wooden catwalk and steps that led to the outhouse and corrals. He smoked briefly, watching Ward as he inspected posts and shook rails around the corral to see if they were still solid. Ward unloaded the horses. After ferrying in coolers and gun cases, Eric primed the hand pump as Ward had asked him to do. The water had a marvelous crispness to it, bouncing along on his tongue.

The hot afternoon light faded into dusk. The temperature dropped enough for Eric to pull on a polar fleece top. Again he was reminded that he'd never done well with cold weather.

Ward checked and reset mousetraps, started a fire in both stoves, then heated one of Lorraine's meals: creamy chicken dumplings. They ate a silent dinner on nicked and mismatched china. Ward ate with the same grimness and determination he had displayed at breakfast, then went out to check on the horses. Eric assumed this meant he was supposed to clean up, which he did, washing by pouring boiling water from the kettle into the sink. He then went out on the porch for a smoke and to glass the land with his binoculars. His hands were getting cold when Ward called him in.

WARD MOVED the kitchen table directly below a hissing gas lamp. He had stripped down to his T-shirt. Eric saw the pouch that had been hanging up in his gun cabinet now made a lump under the white cotton. Ward took out the map and a pen.

"We're here," he said, pointing towards a spot with the still-capped pen. "And here's where we will hunt," he said, scraping the pen around a large area. "It's called Thompson's Bench. It's a mile wide at the most and nearly three miles long. No motor vehicle access, in theory, anyway, which keeps all those lazy ignoramuses on four-wheelers out. We're going to try a couple spots tomorrow, including right here," he circled an area with his pen. "It's right up against the face of the mountain, as you can see. It's north facing and one steep mother. Good for hiding elk. Only problem is that directly on the other side of this ridge is an old logging road. It's also supposed to be closed to motor vehicle traffic, but people still drive up there. We'll see."

He tapped the end of the pen on the table, then looked up. "We get up at four. Better get your beauty sleep while you can."

Eric looked at his watch. It was barely past eight o'clock. This is when he just started to wake up. He crawled into his sleeping bag, smelling of chemical newness, and closed his eyes, feeling a little ridiculous at the attempt. Ward tossed and turned and got up twice. Eric dozed a little, then awoke, but was fully asleep, however, when the alarm went off. Ward's bedspring creaked as he swung his feet to the floor. He lit a gas lamp, then dressed, then threw some kindling on the fire.

"Watch the fire," Ward ordered, then put the water on for coffee, then left to grain the horses.

He seemed almost cheery as he fried eggs and patties of sausage, sliding pots and pans back and forth on the stove. He wolfed down two eggs and sausage patty sandwiches made with an English muffin heated on the stovetop. He suspiciously eyed Eric sipping coffee and nibbling an English muffin. "You won't even have the strength to pull the trigger if you keep up that fare," he said. "You're going to be so weary in three days you won't be able to drag your glute max out of bed."

"I thought the horses were here to do the work for us."

"Some of it, sure," he said tersely. "Depends on where the elk are. I counted four camps between the Cliff Mountain turn-off and our property. That means pressure on the herd."

He wiped his hands on a paper towel with deliberate strokes, and Eric saw he was about to launch into a plan on how to best everyone else. He went to the stove, lifted the lid, and threw in the paper.

"We may end up going to places so daunting that they scare everyone else off, because that's where the elk will go. They're called hidey holes. The one I'm thinking of is way down in the bottom of that canyon and not all that accessible by horse. We may have to bone our elk out on the spot and pack it back up to a place we can get to it by horseback. So don't count on the beast of burden to do all the work. Why don't you prepare some sustenance while I saddle the horses? I'll need at least three sandwiches to last me through the day. Fill both water bottles."

Then, just as suddenly as he opened up, Ward shut down.

"DON'T silhouette yourself," said Ward abruptly, interrupting his reverie as they sat at the edge of the canyon.

"What?"

"Don't walk so close to the edge. You're making a perfect silhouette against the skyline. Elk haven't got the greatest vision in the world, but they can detect movement from a long way off. Keep close to the timberline."

Ward had walked along the ledge, crouching, until he found a niche in the rocks and tucked his tall frame into it, his back supported by a granite slab. He pulled out his binoculars and began scanning the canyon and the country on the far side. Eric waited, assuming this would take but a few moments. The minutes passed; Ward showed no sign of stopping. Eric recalled the book he'd read about elk hunting declared that glassing, as the author called it, was one of the keys to successful hunting. Feeling like he was aping Ward, Eric, shivering, also pulled out his binoculars.

In a few minutes, Ward asked Eric, in the tone as if speaking to a child: "How many animals have you seen?"

Quiz time. "None."

Ward harrumphed and pointed, not moving his binoculars.

"Look due north. Other side of the canyon. See those two outcrops that look like spires? There's a drainage directly to the right. See that? All right, there's a little clearing, almost a mesa, between those two flattish outcrops and where the creek drops off. Look there and tell me what you see."

Eric stared and stared at the point but saw nothing. He knew there was something there and that Ward was doing this just to humiliate him.

"Don't see much."

"Six elk. Possibly a seventh up the hill in the trees. One bull."

Eric still didn't see anything but, feeling stupid, pretended he did.

"Oh, yeah. Aren't they kind of far away?"

"On the reservation or close to it. Our tags won't cover us there. But, they came up from the canyon, right up that drainage. I can see their tracks. And we *can* hunt down there. Tomorrow, maybe."

Ward took the map out of his pocket, marked the sighting of the elk with a date, then went back to glassing. Eventually, he heaved himself up and walked back to the horses.

AT THE edge of an aspen grove, they paused to examine pockets of elk beds. Eric took pride in noting some of them did not shine with the frost of the surrounding grass, meaning they'd been abandoned only hours ago. Ward hmm'd in curiosity and seemed to pick up the pace, heading in a southeast direction. He brought his horse to a stop and dismounted so he could examine some tracks.

"Pretty fresh."

He flipped the reins over LJ's head and walked in front the horse, looking at the ground, then stopped again when he saw a pile of elk turds. He took off a glove and picked one up, squeezing it. "Only a few hours old."

Then he cocked his head in concern. "They're being pushed out of the beds."

He looked at his watch. "Six forty-five. Those elk should just be easing into the timber now, not leaving. A pile of elk shit a couple hours old means they came in here, tried to bed down, but something made them nervous. They're around, all right, but they'll be jumpy."

Ward turned to Eric and looked directly at him for the first time all morning. "You got a shell handy? Be prepared to dismount and shoot."

Ward stuck his fingers between the girth and LJ's side, tugged, seemed satisfied, then swung back on. Eric knew right where his shell was; he was more concerned about the gun. Ever since he'd seen the elk beds, he'd been worried that somehow the scabbard tucked underneath his right stirrup wasn't the right place for his gun. He hadn't liked this arrangement from the moment Ward set it up in the corral that morning. A rifle in the scabbard meant the scope was subject to constant pressure of his right leg against Bullet's belly. What if this altered the scope's mount on the rifle barrel? Ward had assured him it wouldn't, saying a Kahles scope and rings were Teuton tough. Furthermore he didn't like the idea of piling off Bullet and hastily shooting. Too sloppy.

They rode out of the timber, across a marshy meadow, and into a copse of trees. From around a root-wad came a burst of brown, and something large crashed through the trees. Both horses shied, and Eric felt minor panic at Bullet's sudden movement, the loss of control he hated with horses.

"Hey!" he shouted at Bullet, who had actually already stopped and was watching something to the north.

Eric followed his gaze. A mule deer—so big that Eric first thought it was an elk—bounced through the grass. Fat jiggled under his skin with each springing leap. He only had one antler. Ward, trying to compose himself on a twitching LJ, was watching the deer through his binoculars.

"Whoa, goddamn it, LJ," he barked, then turned to Eric. "That's a big damned deer. Huge. Glad to see he's survived so far."

Ward's voice had the first inflection of enthusiasm Eric had heard in two days. But then he dropped his binoculars down onto his chest and said in his usual dull tone, "When you want your horse to stop, just say 'Whoa.'"

The ground got steeper. Ward led them up through an archipelago of fir islands separated by open meadows. Eric relished the sun's warmth; he'd been cold since they mounted up. His right knee was beginning to throb. They were in the trees, close to the edge of a long, narrow meadow that led like a runway to the ridge, when Ward suddenly pulled back on LJ's reins and quickly dismounted. "Elk. Top of the ridge, right at the edge of the timber. Get your rifle and load up. I'll tie up Bullet. Keep yourself concealed."

Eric did as instructed, his mind racing, exploring the possibilities. He rapidly came to the conclusion that it wouldn't work in this situation. Ward would be right beside him, wouldn't he? *Putain de bordel*, he swore to himself. Would the time ever come?

Eric put the range finder to his eyes. Over 300 yards away, restless elk milled around in a pocket of grass and rock. Some walked into the timber, single file. A cluster, mostly cows, hesitated and stared at something off on the south tip of the ridge. Ward came up from behind and squatted down.

"Something's up there," he pronounced immediately in a whisper.

"What?" said Eric, again feeling inept.

"Something's got their attention. I'll bet some son of a bitch has come up the back of the ridge with an ATV. Where's your range finder? What's the yardage?"

Before Eric could answer, a volley of gunshots, loud booms, one after the other, roared down the hill. Eric jolted in alarm, dropping the range finder so it bounced off his chest when it hit the end of the lanyard.

There was a thwack, thwack of bullets hitting elk flesh. One cow fell immediately and did not move. Another wheeled down the hill, running crazily, directionless, then collapsed face first in the grass. Then she tried to get up again, but couldn't and lay there, head up, looking dazed. A cow and a spike, his foot-long horns sticking up like toothpicks, staggered around. The cow pulled herself along, dragging her rear legs. The spike had his front leg shot off and was trying to make it into the timber in a drunken, staggering walk. The shots kept coming. The second cow went down. The spike persisted, however, and his yellow rump was swallowed up by the trees. Then the shooting stopped. A chorus of cheers and whistles came from the ridge.

Engine sounds. Two four-wheelers came over the ridge at high RPM'S. One man, he looked more like a boy, ran beside them, carrying his rifle by his side. The first wounded cow tried to get up and run, but collapsed. The boy stopped, jacked a round into the rifle, and started shooting at her. He aimed practically right at Ward and Eric. The bullets whizzed by, singing their pernicious song. One splintered a tree not twenty yards away.

Ward immediately backed up in a crouch, grabbing Eric by the elbow. "Shit! Stupid bastard. He doesn't even see us! Let's bail," he said.

They ran back to the horses, who were swishing their tails in anxiety. LJ tossed his head up and down. Ward quickly untied their lead ropes, handed one to Eric, and led them deep into the timber.

"Welcome to hunting on public ground," he muttered, his face dark with anger.

They hunted the remainder of the morning in listless silence. Around eleven, they stopped for lunch, although Eric wasn't particularly hungry. Ward took the headstalls off the horses, loosened their girths, and hobbled them both. LJ protested and Ward swore at him impatiently. The horses clumped off to find green grass.

"Think they'll ever find that spike elk?" asked Eric after a while, listening to the horses rip up grass. He wished he could forget trauma as easily as they could.

"Hard to say. Had a lot of lead in him. He'll most likely lie down and die. Elk are very tough. Just hope those dumb fucks can read a blood trail." He tossed his half-eaten sandwich to a predatory gray jay, who'd been sitting on the lower branches of a fir, waiting. "It gets worse every year."

In the afternoon, Ward led them to the easternmost parcel of Thompson's Bench. It had actually gotten hot, and dark patches of sweat appeared on Bullet's neck. They moved into scrubby aspen and old clearcuts thick with new lodgepole pine. It was harder going, and the horses had to move slowly, stepping over blow-downs and circumventing thickets. They saw old tracks and scat, but no elk. They got on a deeply rutted logging road, fresh four-wheeler tire marks evident, before they startled two men, covered head-to-toe in orange, sitting on a log, smoking. One raised his gun halfway, then put it down, smirking in embarrassment.

Ward turned the horses around. "Sooner or later Bullet and LJ will be mistaken for elk. Let's clear the hell out of here."

———

THAT EVENING a frightening debility took over Eric. He felt a paralyzing fatigue. His inner legs trembled and throbbed. A pain in his right leg forced him to walk with a limp. He again envied Ward and his ability with horses. He had those long legs, for starters, that swung over the top of LJ's back with ease, not catching on the saddle bags, as Eric's legs seemed to do each time he mounted and dismounted.

More worrisome to Eric than weariness or bodily aches was the fate of his grand plan. Thus far, none of the elk sightings and potential shooting opportunities had proceeded as envisioned.

His mind eased when Ward got out the maps after dinner. Flattening one on the table he said, "We were going to hunt around the cabin for two days. The elk are here. But so are other hunters. S-o-o-o..."

He paused. "We're going down into the canyon tomorrow. It's a heads-up show, Lindsay. Involves some very steep ground. You're going to have to pay better attention. You were daydreaming in the saddle today. Don't assume Bullet's going to babysit you all the time."

Ward got up and tossed his bowl into the sink, then went outside and spent a long time in the corral.

That night Eric lay in bed, exhausted, but unable to sleep, his brain buzzing like a transformer, going over the task that lay ahead. Suddenly he felt his inner animal rise with such force it took his breath away. Its vigor frightened him.

When he pushed against it, it pushed back tauntingly.

CHAPTER 6

THEY RODE IN THE DARK, Eric stiff and sore and hoping the ibuprofen would kick in. He felt a little better, but another day of this and he'd be on his last membrane of will. He wore his Olathes and hoped they would not have to walk much. They followed the remains of an old logging road. When it was barely light, Ward paused, backtracked for five minutes, then turned directly into the woods. Back in the dark again, they made slow detours over or around downed timber. They rode with their heads down, avoiding branches. Ward hesitated several times as if attempting to get his bearings. They hit a game trail and the riding improved. Then the trail became very steep. Eric let Bullet pick and feel his way.

At a small bench, Ward got off.

"It's about to get seriously steep. Too hard on the horses to have somebody on their back. Take 'er slow and easy. Let the horses find their way down."

They eased down the trail leading the horses, making short zig-zags across rocky, gravelly soil and scree, the animals grunting in exertion. Eric's feet began to ache, but he was grateful for the steep packer's heels of his cowboy boots; they dug into the hillside and helped him keep his balance. *How am I going to get two horses back up here by myself?* he wondered. Then he chided himself not to worry about the future. After what seemed an eternity, the ground began to level. His boot heels dug into earth, not gravel, and the trees began getting bigger. Running water took over the hissing in his ears.

At the edge of a clearing, Ward stopped to glass. Eric turned and looked up at where they had just come down. He wouldn't have believed such a descent possible if he hadn't just done it. By the time it was fully light, they were deep in a canyon. Ward stopped again and looked at the map, then up at the wall on the other side of the canyon.

"One of my favorite spots in the world."

"How did you find it?"

"One year I tracked a big bull down here in the snow. That's how I found that passage down. Following tracks. Ended up losing him because there were so many tracks down here I couldn't tell which were his."

"Can I smoke?"

Ward shook his head.

"Where are we?"

"About right here," Ward circled the worn map with a gloved hand.

"Beyond that I don't know. The township and range are just approximations on this chunk of ground. And I can say with a reasonable degree of confidence that the topo lines in this drainage are in error. I don't know—for absolute certain—if we're in Wyoming or the reservation."

The sun came out. Eric felt warm enough to join Ward in peeling off his jacket and tying it to the saddle strings before they went farther into the canyon. They went down into a side drainage and up the other side until the ground got too steep and rocky. They dismounted and walked. They stopped at the top to let the horses blow then remounted and rode through a flat bench, a thin peninsula of timber, until Ward abruptly swung off LJ and hurriedly put a half-hitch around a shrub. He silently went ahead on foot, binoculars in one hand. By his urgency, Eric knew something was up.

"Thought I saw something below us."

Bending down on one knee, Ward braced against a tree and stared though the glasses down to the canyon bottom.

"Legs and hair. They're down in that clump of trees. Next to the water. See?" He whispered. "A little pod of them. They know something's up but they can't quite figure it out."

This time Eric had no trouble finding the elk. Ward peered through the binoculars again.

"If they head down the drainage we're screwed. However, if they come east up this little draw right in front of us, you should be able to get a respectable shot."

He dropped his binoculars and looked at Eric.

"I'll tell you what. I'm going to ride back the way we came. Then I'll drop down into that north-facing draw we passed and come around those elk on the east side. I'm going to try and get a shot, too, but they'll probably catch my scent. They should come right this way. You'll be able to see me going down the hill over there. All right?"

"All right." Eric felt his pulse climb.

"Breathe and be steady. Get yourself a rifle rest on that downed fir over there. Your tag allows either cow or bull. Make a nice clean shot."

He slapped Eric gently on the shoulder.

"I know you will."

He swung up on LJ and, without looking back, rode off through the trees ducking branches.

Eric tied up Bullet. He extracted the rifle from the scabbard then got out the ammunition and range finder from the saddlebags. He walked over to a fallen fir, his hands shaking, but mind focused. He took out a shell and set it on the log beside the range finder and rifle. He squatted with the binoculars and looked at the clump of trees. The elk were still there; a cow and calf were outside the group, grazing. Eric swung his binoculars around. To the west, he saw Ward's orange hat flashing through the trees, then disappear. A few minutes later, Ward reappeared at an opening just behind an aspen tree almost shorn of leaves and tied up his horse. Eric took a sighting on Ward's back with the range finder: 277 yards. His hands still shook. Too far. Ward went behind a small ridge and came out on the other side, half-crouching, his rifle slung on his back and binoculars up. Eric took another reading: 174 yards. Acceptable distance. He reached for the Ruger.

Shoving down the action, he slipped a cartridge into the chamber and closed the lever with a snap. He lifted up the rifle and looked through the scope only to see Ward disappear. A chilling voice immediately chided him for missed opportunities. There was nothing remotely congenial about the tone. Before, the voice within had moved him not only by its power, but by solidarity of purpose, the voice of one wise being to another. Now it had the feel of an imperial, sizzling cattle prod.

Eric turned, his breathing shallow and harsh. Don't let that happen again. A cloud seemed to hover momentarily around his brain. He took a series of diaphragm-controlled deep breaths, then worked his way on his knees over to the downed fir, the clean acrid odor of needles acting as smelling salts, refocusing his mind. He glanced through the binoculars. More elk had come out from the timber, but they were still and looking in one direction, presumably towards Ward. A cow twitched her ears and, to Eric's surprise, barked like dog. She then began to move up the hill at a trot. The other elk followed and disappeared into the bottom of the draw. How would he get to shoot Ward?

Then a plan appeared just as smoothly as every other detail of this venture had appeared when necessary. Eric took a deep breath of relief, knowing he would not be thwarted. He would shoot an elk as planned, killing it, but not move from his shooting spot. Ward, ever responsible, would immediately go to the downed animal. When he bent down to inspect it, Eric would put a 180-grain bullet through his temple.

He pulled an additional shell out of the ammunition carrier, set it on the log, and focused the range finder on the top of the draw.

The elk, if they stayed on route, should come out at 110 yards away. Perfect. The diaphragm breathing slowed his heartbeat; his hands only shook a little. He nestled down behind the pine. He waited and tucked the butt of the rifle snugly against his shoulder. They should make an appearance at any time.

He felt remarkably clear-headed, with none of the brackish taste on his tongue that accompanied thoughts of Ward. He had sudden access to events: carrying Gwen's casket in an unseasonably cold October rain in Valentine, tromping with sopping shoes through a forest of bleached marble tombstones; a train going by in the middle of the funeral, the roaring and clacking drowning out the preacher's words; his father, already on the way down, slipping in the mud, hitting his chin on the corner of the car door, slicing him open, requiring stitches, spilling blood down the front of his raincoat.

A scalding rage moved through him, filling his muscles with a cold fire.

Eric squinted into the scope. Coming out of the top of the draw was not an elk, but Ward, slightly bent from the exertion of climbing the hill. He wasn't carrying his rifle. Where are the elk? Eric wondered. What the fuck was Ward doing? The voice inside, however, jabbed him with an ice pick. *No time for silly queries. He's right there. Shoot him. Now.* Eric peered through the scope again. Ward wasn't looking his direction or paying the slightest bit of attention to his presence. He's acting like I'm not even here, thought Eric.

Ward sat down on a rock and turned his back to him. Eric squinted into the scope. The crosshairs wobbled on the back of Ward's hat brim. He couldn't bear to shoot and miss. Then, to his surprise, Ward took off his hat and rested it on his knee, then turned halfway toward Eric, looking up the canyon and was still. He looked like a child gazing up at the flag during the recitation of the Pledge of Allegiance.

Then Eric didn't feel so much surprised as dumbfounded. Ward was waiting for Eric to kill him.

Suddenly he was afraid. His sense of confidence vanished and the inner animal that had goaded him for the last six months took leave, like a cowardly ringleader who plans but does not act. Still, he must carry this out. Eric squinted though the scope again and flicked off the safety. Ward did not move.

A magpie above him squawked, and he flinched, almost pulling the trigger. *Shut up!* he wanted to scream, then thought—wouldn't that be tragic? I squander my chance to settle a score because a black-and-white bird shatters my concentration. Ward continued to sit, not moving his head or shoulders. Directly to the north, Eric heard the elk talking to each other, the high squeaks and chirps of the cows and calves. Their conversation came from the base of a magnificent sandstone wall. Apparently they'd gone up a different draw. Then he wondered if Ward had led him to this spot, knowing the elk would find an escape route and provide an opportunity for Eric to perform his task.

The concept that Ward would orchestrate his own killing had never, even for an instant, figured in Eric's plans. Instead of a sharp, neat conclusion that brought on triumph, he felt his sensation of victory slide away, slowly at first, then rushing, like the collapse of a dam on a swollen river. He no longer felt cunning or clever, but excruciatingly foolish, a sensation he could never stand; the heat of the humiliation almost made him jerk his finger back. But, like the samurai who refused to execute a man who had spit in his face because killing in anger would desecrate honor, to shoot Ward due to a flaring temper would despoil all.

Eric had been beaten at his own game. Beyond beaten. Failure to carry this through was the ultimate affirmation of what he felt that day at the Berkeley reunion—his life was through. He must shoot Ward or shoot himself. If he could not pull the trigger, he must find another way to live. But he could not let himself die in this condition.

He pointed the .308 into the air and fired into a blue sky. He neither felt the recoil nor heard the booming sound. Then he ran at

Ward, scrambling, falling, skinning his knees, picking himself back up. He planned to strike Ward in back of the head with his rifle butt and maybe kill him that way, but he found himself unable to do even that. Ward remained stationary as a statue. Eric tackled him like a child tackling a bigger brother sitting among leaves. Then Eric began to strike him. Neck. Ears. Back. Forehead. Ward made no attempt to protect himself. Eric struck him in the nose with all his might. Ward's head bounced and his eyes went wide. When Eric saw Ward's nose gush with blood, his anger, his will to vanquish, disappeared. He pulled out a handkerchief and held it against his friend's nostrils. A great welling noise, utterly involuntary in origin, roared up Eric's throat, like the wailing of a mother over her infant's coffin. It echoed through the drainage, eventually being absorbed by the porous sandstone, dark timber, and a bank of gray clouds now coming over the canyon.

Ward finally moved, getting up on one elbow and putting his other arm around him and said in voice unsophisticated and plain, a trembling voice of twenty-five years ago, the voice of a Berkeley sophomore.

"I'm sorry, Eric. About Gwen. I'm so, so sorry."

Eric dropped his head, no longer having the strength to hold it up. Neither did he have the power to speak, all the thousands of words he had floating around in his cranial channels, but all he could utter was, "Okay. It's okay."

BEING ON horseback helped keep the demons at bay. When you feel the lowest of the low, a horse will tell you you are all right. The tight sensation of a saddle beneath him and sunlight and wind seemed to shield him, envelop him in a protective wrapper. It kept Ward from whiskey and steered his mind away from five consecutive years of bad cattle prices. Yet, the short days of fall were a harbinger of winter, the season of struggle.

After the brief snowstorm of a week ago, Josh had inquired, "Well, Dad, are you ready for winter?" As if any soul had a choice.

Even in sunny October and in the presence of Eric Lindsay, his resistance to depression evaporated. It was akin to a single nimble sword fighter, rapier flashing, trying to hold off a score of seasoned, well-armored, determined mercenaries wielding battle axes and cudgels. Eventually, their blows brought him down.

Tending the horses that morning in the dark outside the cabin, listening to them grind their grain with their molars, serenaded by a great northern owl hooting for its mate, Ward knew the time had come. Some desperations gnaw out your insides like the work of the ichneumon wasp, saving the vital parts for last. When they collapse, it's over. Witnessing the previous day's elk slaughter pushed him into the abyss. Filled with lead, mortally wounded but for some reason still standing, that spike needed a place to go die alone.

Ward knew that no love, not that of Lorraine or his boys or his horses, would save him this time. It was infantile to keep relying on some outer authority. Only he, no spouse or therapist or chemical or divine power could deliver the critical goods. He knew then, standing below a quartet of old Douglas fir that had managed to survive disease, fire, and drought, that he could not.

His brain ached with a sensation that defied description, a hopelessness, a feeling he had felt since the moment he heard the roar of that shotgun over a quarter of a century ago.

A few years back, right in the middle of swathing the first cutting of alfalfa, he'd raced back to the diesel tanks beside the barn to refuel. He also wanted to add more iced tea to his thermos. In the kitchen, the beginnings of a stew simmered on the stove; Lorraine was gone, but he thought nothing of it. A thousand chores could have taken her anywhere. But as he returned to the idling swather, he noticed the door to his office was ajar. He went to shut it and found Lorraine, wearing an apron, sitting on the floor with a book in her hand. The sight was so incongruous that he was speechless. She only went into his office to clean or to plop down a stack of bills on the tray marked RANCH STUFF—BILLS DUE. His books never merited more than a passing interest for her.

She looked up when she heard him. Her face was wet and at first he stupidly thought it was sweat. Then he saw the pattern of tears. She held up a book of Paul Tillich's essays.

"These words," she said, "came from God. Of course, a man wrote it, but he was just a vehicle for God's love. Listen." She looked at Ward and read from the book, her voice quavering and lower lip trembling, that "'one must muster the courage to accept oneself as accepted in spite of being unacceptable.'"

"That's you, Ward," she said. "This man, whoever he is, speaks your sophisticated language, but he's saying the same things I do in my plain tongue. Can you hear him?"

Then she got off the floor and ran to him and flung herself into his arms, crying loudly, her shoulders shaking, until one of the twins wandered in, drawn to the open door, looking for someone to show how'd he'd made a cat's cradle out of orange baling twine.

Ward retreated to the swather, forgetting his thermos of tea on the study windowsill, wondering how, among his thousands of books, she had managed to pull that down from the shelf and read that passage.

Tillich was right. Lorraine was right. But the idea of living a life contaminated by such carelessness was not acceptable no matter how he tried to make it so.

When Eric had shown up with that .308—a sniper rifle camouflaged in glorious walnut—and shot twice into the same hole at the rifle range, Ward felt a chill go through him. Now he must face his fate with calm, the way the French aristocracy did during the revolution, when, as one Spanish philosopher said, they accepted the guillotine the way a tumor accepted the lancet.

The only marginal control he had was when and where, a choice, he mused, shared by so few people in this world. How lucky he was.

Riding in the early morning dark, Ward feared he wouldn't find the game trail to the canyon floor. The country at the north end of the Bighorns was famous for getting people turned around. There were stories about how canyons had swallowed sheep and sheep-herder for days. A fearful anxiety pervaded him that he would get lost and not receive what he must. The feeling did not abate until he was at the bottom of the canyon.

When he spotted that small herd clustered in the trees, a warm, easy, feeling close to that of euphoria flooded his brainpan. The elk had winded him as planned and headed straight for a narrow draw, a small fold in the north canyon wall that evaded all but the familiar eye.

Climbing the short hill to place himself within Lindsay's rifle range, Ward felt lighter and lighter, oxygen supplemented instead of deprived, and a great weight rose. Thoughts of Lorraine, the boys, and the MK did not enter into his mind; rather there was the anticipation of blessed alleviation. He did not entertain the slightest worry that Lindsay would miss.

He could not see Eric off to his left, but he knew he was there, hidden among the trees, snug against the fallen fir, breathing steadily. It would make it easier on both parties if he did not face his killer, but instead engage a halfway pose, looking up the canyon. That would be a fine last vision.

When he heard the shot and felt nothing, his first thought was: *He missed. How odd.* He didn't quite believe it. Then he heard the running footsteps and did not know what to think, other than he must stay put and let matters unfold and take whatever came next.

A desperate sense of disappointment arose when Eric tackled him. He wanted to shout: *No. No. No! This won't secure my release.* But when Lindsay struck him in the nose, the physical sensation and pain jarred him. Something deep within moved, almost imperceptibly, although he could not say exactly what it was or identify the source. Then he remembered his father recalling once how a Marine drill sergeant in basic training had hit him in the face, slapped him in exasperation at his false confidence. "It was the slap that changed me," his father had said. "The physical sensation woke me up, broke my pride, and saved my life. From that day on, I knew my silver tongue wasn't anything but dross unless I put action behind my words."

Ward could not pull the wagon of guilt any farther. He alone must forgive his actions and not beg the pity of God or Lindsay or Lorraine. The more he asked for contrition of others, the darker his blackness. Then, paradoxically, when Lindsay held a handkerchief up to his bleeding nose, when someone was offering aid, the brother of Gwen, he felt his desperate sense to die fade. He knew that he must repeat those words that he'd said the day of the accident, but now must say them again, out loud, to himself, for himself. *Sorry. Sorry. Sorry.*

CHAPTER 7

THEY HUNTED DOWN THE CANYON, seeing fresh tracks in the sandy bottom but no elk. They spoke little, both afraid that once they started, there would be no stopping the torrent.

The canyon dropped in elevation. Walls rose and the bottom narrowed. The horses faltered, shoes skidding on over rocks. They stopped.

Ward said he'd never explored this far down but he was sure they were in Montana and on the reservation. His voice resumed the warmth it had when Eric first arrived at the MK. The dark eyes relaxed under the brim of his hat. A blue bruise surrounded one eye and his upper lip had ballooned.

"The Crow, with good reason, don't take kindly to non–tribal members hunting their elk."

Eric rolled a cigarette while Ward studied the map for a long time, then said, "I think we're right here."

They turned around and found a drainage leading south out of the canyon creek, but no trail.

"Could that be Jack Creek? Ah, the fact is I don't know where the hell we are. Let's try going up here anyway. It's the right direction."

They endured a hard two-hour side-hill stumbling climb, leading the horses over and around downed trees, rock slides, ledges, and thick stands of stunted timber. The slick soles of the Olathes held no ground. They stopped often to rest, and once Ward stopped so abruptly that Eric almost ran into him.

The space in Eric's world previously obsessed with sanguine thoughts now stood empty and confused to the point of non-function. A suppurating wound had been punctured; but the opportunity to heal confused his brain. It spun like a gyroscope in the presence of the void. Debilitating sensations of heart-pounding anxiety accompanied these feelings. It came in waves, flushing his cheeks, then flattened out, only to reappear ten minutes later.

His ability to partition regret or any unpleasant sensation had always stood him in good stead. But from the moment they had passed Tommy Yellow Legs's house two days previous, Eric had battled a growing sense of vulnerability: someone out there would decipher his deed. He could not shake the possibility that a tracker, born into this country, might review the crime scene and be asked to offer an opinion on Eric's version of events. He would be discovered and hounded and punished.

Ward stopped suddenly and flipped the lead rope over the horse's withers.

"Smell that?" Ward whispered.

Eric put his nose to the wind like a bird dog. A musky odor met his nostrils, a smell not unlike a feedlot, but with a slightly sweeter tinge. He nodded his head. Ward said in an excited whisper:

"That's elk. And they are *close*. Tie up Bullet. Get your rifle ready and follow me."

He raised his eyebrows like an excited kid, then got his own rifle out of the scabbard and slung it across his back. He put his binoculars up and scanned the trees.

"Nothing yet," he said in a hushed voice. "The wind is most decidedly in our favor."

Ward slowly pushed through the trees, walked a few steps, then stopped and dropped his binoculars, startling Eric with loud chuckling laughter.

"Fooled. Look here."

Ward pushed aside a clump of doghair Douglas fir. Twenty yards away stood a mud hole that a man could walk through in about five paces. A little basin of dusky water collected at the bottom of the shallow indentation. In the circumference around the pool, hundreds of elk hoofprints had churned up black earth. Elk hair, fir needles, and leaves sprouted from the mud hole; it emanated musk to the point of stink. Flies and mosquitoes buzzed their heads and the horses tossed and stomped in irritation.

"It's a wallow," said Ward, "fed by a little seep. Bulls piss in here then roll around. Makes them feel studly. A wallow indicates we're in elk central. Never knew this was here. Then again, our exact location remains a mystery."

He looked at Eric and asked in a voice of genuine concern. "You look a little pale, pilgrim. How you feeling?"

"Tired."

"Me, too." Then he laughed. "Close to exhausted. How're your feet?"

"Sore. So are my ankles. These boots aren't worth a shit going uphill."

"I know. Should be easier going from now on. Wallows usually have a pretty decent trail leading to them, and this hillside will level out pretty quickly. We'll be able to ride soon. How're you and Bullet making out?"

Ward walked over and stroked Bullet's muzzle.

"Okay, I guess. I haven't hit the ground yet."

"Eric, I think this horse actually likes you. You want to rest a bit more? How's your water supply?"

"It's fine. No, I'll be okay," said Eric, although he wanted to lie down in the cool patch of salal and stare at the tree canopy, listen to the soothing sounds of Stan Getz or Paul Desmond, and reassess the events of the day. But he did not think: *What am I going to do now?* No planning or scheming or questions about the future. He was strangely content. Then he realized that the pressure, that mounting pressure from inside his head, was gone. Completely vanished.

"Well, let's push on, if you're feeling up to it. Carry your gun if you can. We can stop anytime you want. Have a shell ready. I suspect we're going to see something soon."

Trails networked the wallows heading south and west. Ward found a path that more or less followed one direction and walked ahead, leading his horse and carrying his rifle. Eric felt relief at following a trail, wandering as it was, simple relief that he could follow and be grateful for it. He watched Ward move slowly, walking in small steps and hesitating to glass. Eric wondered what Ward was thinking.

The wind picked up and rushed through the tops of the trees. The temperature dropped and a rawness sank into his damp clothes, drying the sweat on Eric's neck. He felt cold and wondered if Ward also experienced the chill. It didn't look like he did. But a new slump in Ward's shoulders told Eric that Ward was indeed tired. Eventually, Ward stopped walking completely, hitched his rifle strap up on his shoulder, and exhaled in mild exasperation.

"Oh hell," he said, as if he were speaking to himself. "I know exactly where we are. We're about to come out on top of a ridge that's east of the cabin. We're going to hit an old logging road soon. Why didn't I figure this out sooner?"

Then he took out the map, extracted a pen from his shirt pocket and, putting the map up on the saddle, scribbled a mark on the green paper. He bent down and picked a dried stalk of grass and held it up. Eric untied his jacket from the back of the saddle and put it on. Ward did the same.

"Wind's still blowing in our favor. Carries a chill, though. The weather's sure changed. Feels like we might even get some snow."

They walked for long spell without glassing or stopping, then Ward veered off the trail, leading them to a pair of young fir.

"This is elky territory. Let's tie up and walk slowly towards that opening in the trees up there. We need to stop every twenty yards or so and glass. You go first."

"No. Go ahead," said Eric.

"You've got to shoot an elk."

"Ah, I don't have to, really," said Eric who was feeling tentative about pulling the trigger on anything. He wanted to find that canyon rim and hurl the rifle over the edge.

Ward looked at him steadily and said. "No, Lindsay. For me. For you. For both of us. You need to shoot an elk."

"Your tone sounds suspiciously pedagogical, Fall. You sure you haven't been teaching on the sly?"

"Not me, pilgrim."

Eric found himself able to breathe easier. The ground was more open. Gone were the thickets found only 500 yards below them. In their stead were small communities of ankle-high plants interspersed by mostly lodgepole pine. Eric looked through his binoculars at the opening ahead.

Nothing but grass and a few solitary trees he said to himself.

He pressed on, hearing LJ's footsteps close behind him. Eric stopped and put his binoculars up to his glasses but almost let them fall to his chest when he noticed a slight movement between two ponderosa pines. He put the glasses up again. Brown hair.

"Ward?" he whispered.

Ward looked at him attentively.

"Check out two big pines down there. I see something between them. Hair. Does it belong to a deer or an elk?"

Ward walked abreast of him and looked. "Why, that's elk hair. Nice job of glassing. I looked right there twenty seconds ago and saw nothing. Slip a shell into your trusty .308."

Eric hesitated.

"Go ahead. I'll mind Bullet."

Eric had not replaced the backup shell originally scheduled to split open Ward's skull. Instead, he'd slipped it into his Filsons. He felt its smooth shape protruding outside his pants, along with the casing of the shell intended to kill that spectral cow climbing out of the draw. He reached in and extracted the cartridge and felt its retention of his body heat. It slid into the cold receiver that he closed with a clack. He slipped on the safety.

"It's a cow," Ward whispered, his eyes still glued to the binoculars. "And it looks like she's all by herself. She feeding and doesn't have an inkling we're here."

"Would you take the shot from here?" asked Eric.

"Up to you," said Ward. "That can't be more than one hundred fifty yards, and for a guy who drilled a one-inch group, that target's a piece of cake."

"What if I move up just a bit and use that low-hanging branch over there as a rest?"

"Sounds like a plan. Just be sure you've got a clear shot. Wait."

Ward set down his binoculars and fumbled around his neck. He extracted the pouch from under his shirt and took it off his neck. He held it out.

"Wear this."

"But that's yours."

"It is and it isn't."

"Explain, please."

"Later. Put it on, shut up, and shoot."

Eric bent his head down and Ward slipped the bag over his neck. Eric tucked it next to his skin; he could feel Ward's sweat. How many damp chests had felt this leather? Ward put up his binoculars and peered into the opening.

"She's still there. Head down and feeding."

Eric crept up to an ancient spruce, the largest tree in sight, and set his rifle across a branch close to the trunk. He could smell the tree's pitch and, despite a strong wind, reveled in the solidity of the trunk. The scaly bark bit pleasantly into his right shoulder, holding him steady. He looked through the scope. The cow was broadside, looking directly at him. He froze, figuring he'd been seen, but she dropped her head and continued feeding. Her sense of ease had obviously gone; she kept looking up.

Ward said, as if reading his thoughts: "She's a little suspicious.

The wind's whirling around a bit and she might have gotten a whiff of us."

"I don't like this."

Ward looked at him and said in an even, low whisper. "Just do your job and she won't suffer."

At first Eric thought he heard the same old lecturing Ward, but there was almost a pleading to his voice, the voice of a pastor imploring one of the flock to come to the altar and be saved.

The cow took a step forward. She dropped her head again.

He put the crosshairs right above the shoulder joint, pushed the gun off safety, and breathed twice to still his thumping heart, then gently squeezed the trigger on an outtake of breath.

Dried spruce needles trickled to earth. The cow jerked her head up, startled, and stepped quickly forward as if nothing had happened. How could he have missed? Why did he heed Ward?

"Got her," said Ward, "You got her. Heard the bullet strike." But Eric wasn't listening. He ran, stumbling, lungs burning from lack of air, skidding down the hill to reach the place where the animal had stood. Gone. He looked at the ground. No blood. He turned and looked in the direction the cow had trotted off. No animal. He followed her vague tracks up over a little rise, then saw her lying on her side in a knick-knick–covered hummock, head resting at the base of a tree. She seemed very big. Right in back of her shoulder blade was a barely visible puncture. The bullet had gone exactly where he thought it should. Her jaw went up and down but the eyes carried the glazed-over patina of the dead.

Ward slowly followed him, leading the horses.

"Nice shot."

"She ran. Her jaw's still moving. Look. Her leg just flinched."

"Tough critters. Don't worry. She's dead. They just don't keel over like you think they should. Just like that spike. Well, now the fun begins. Here, hold these horses while I get some gear out and hobble them."

Eric grabbed the reins but continued to stare at the elk while

Ward loosened both girths. From his saddlebags Ward took out two sets of hobbles, a saw, two knives, a down vest, and a sharpening stone. From Eric's saddlebag he extracted the canvas panniers and game bags. He put down the tools, pulled on the vest, then put the hobbles first on Bullet, who stood patiently, then LJ, who again resisted having the leather straps put around his front legs. Finally Ward took the bridles off and hung them on a broken branch. Both horses dropped their heads and immediately began to graze.

"I'm famished, too," said Ward, speaking directly to the horses. "I require a quick fix of tucker before we address this cow. How about you, Lindsay?"

Eric didn't think he could eat if his life depended on it. Puking was not out of the question.

"Lost my appetite."

Ward shrugged and dug into one of Bullet's saddlebags for a sandwich. "Suit yourself. You always this reluctant to gain nourishment? I recall you not being much of a gourmand at Berkeley, but I bet you haven't consumed two thousand calories in two days."

"Being in the presence of a freshly killed creature does not usually stimulate one's gastric juices, Fall."

"Guess you have a point. Cup of coffee at least?"

"I could do that."

Ward tossed him the thermos then speedily consumed a sausage-and-cheese sandwich. He held the sandwich in one hand while gingerly thumbing knife blades with the other. He held one up to Eric, handle first.

"Want to gut her? Don't be afraid to say no. Be happy to do it."

Eric swallowed the last of the lukewarm coffee, relishing the heat as it went down his esophagus. It made him feel better.

"I'll try."

"Okay," said Ward enthusiastically, as if one of his young sons had agreed to take on calculus. "Roll up your sleeves. Take off your watch. Lemme start it for you, just to be sure we don't puncture the guts."

"Sure."

"Here. Stand over there and hold her front legs apart."

Eric did as asked. With the very tip of his knife, Ward began slicing shallow cuts into the hide above mid-belly; he repeatedly went over one area. Hair flew in little brittle threads, and when a bit of white fatty tissue appeared, he grabbed the hide with one hand, then flipped the knife over, so it was blade-side up, and gently pushed it in at an angle while simultaneously pulling the hide up with his other hand. The knife sank in about an inch.

"Bingo. She's all yours. Slice down to just short of that little excuse for an udder. She's young and dry, an unusual combination. Must be the power of that pouch."

"Mind if I use my own knife?"

"If it's sharp, sure.

"How did you get that pouch, by the way?"

"I traded it with an old Northern Cheyenne woman for a side of beef and a couple packages of elk meat. Gladys Walks Around. It belonged to her great-great uncle, a formidable hunter and warrior, I am told. By tradition, an artifact like that goes to somebody in her clan. But she's on the outs with them. She didn't have sons and she can't stand any of her sons-in-law. Too lazy to hunt. Or if they did, they don't bring her back any meat and that pissed her off incredibly. She told me the pouch should be worn by a hunter. Didn't matter what color his skin was."

Slowly, inch-by-inch, Eric sliced open the cow until the stomach wall protruded like a swollen balloon. He got as far as the udder then stopped. He went to the other side of the opening and began cutting towards the throat.

"Did the pouch come empty?"

"It did."

Ward held the front legs as Eric ran the knife tip over the ribby brisket, pulled back the hide, then sawed up the breastbone.

"What did you put in it?"

"It contains, if I recall, a bullet found at Buster's Cattlefield, as we like to say around here, a claw from a red-tailed hawk, a braid of wolverine fur, one of my mother's emerald-and-diamond earrings—she lost the other one in Monte Carlo—a magpie's tail feather, a front tooth from each one of the twins, and, let's see, a twist of Lorraine's pubic hair."

Eric stopped sawing and looked up. "You're kidding me about that last one."

"I am not. Hunting pouches require strong female power. And for reasons not totally comprehended by yours truly, this talisman works. It's an equal opportunity employer. Look. Here's proof."

With both hands, Ward opened the steaming chest cavity and reached in and pulled out with bloody hands the heart still intact but with the arch of the aorta severed.

"See? Just missed the heart but a deadly shot nonetheless."

Ward reached over and with his right thumb imprinted a bloody mark on Eric's forehead. "Got to have first-kill blood." Ward looked at him. "Kind of looks like one of those spots Hindus decorated themselves with, a tilak, right?"

"Your guess is as good as mine."

"Thought you'd know for sure. Didn't you take a swing at Asian philosophy? Don't the old swamis say that an application of a tilak frees one from all duality?" said Ward. "Do I remember that correctly? Of course, a good Hindu Brahman would rather eat a T-bone with an untouchable than wear a tilak concocted out of elk blood, I suppose, wouldn't he? What are they usually made out of, anyway?"

"Sandalwood. Powdered sandalwood," Eric suddenly and improbably remembered, reaching up to feel the dried blood.

"Ah-ha. Sandalwood, naturally. Well, we're a little short on that commodity in the Bighorns. Elk blood will have to do."

Sawing through the pelvic bone took time. Ward showed him how to keep the saw shallow so as to avoid popping the bladder. He helped Eric cut around the anus, freeing up the flopping, pellet-filled intestine from the surrounding tissue.

"There. Now the rest is easy."

They swung the elk around to allow gravity to help them. Ward cut the trachea where the neck met the skull, then punctured a hole through both sides, like putting a pencil through a cardboard tube. He put two fingers through holes.

"I'll pull. You cut. Careful not to carve into the backstrap as you cut away from the backbone."

Warm blood soaked him up to his elbows and spilled out on his Filsons. Slowly, methodically, they cut and pulled the viscera from the carcass. He tried not to breathe through his mouth. When the entrails were completely removed, Ward dragged them away, referring to them as a smorgasbord for the coyotes. Ward wiped his hands on the grass and took out another knife, one with a short, stubby blade. He felt the edge and hummed in approval.

"Save the hide?"

Eric shrugged indifferently. He couldn't imagine what he'd do with it. "Doesn't matter."

"Why don't we go ahead and skin her? You might think of a use later. I've got game bags to protect the meat. I'll need your help, though."

Eric held the elk, watching as Ward, using the short-bladed skinning knife, deftly separated the skin from the tissue, most of which he seemed to pull off rather than cut. The carcass looked small and clinical with the hide off, not quite so intimidating. Ward flipped the animal and stripped out the tenderloin from under the backbone, which he put into a ziplock bag he had stashed in a sad-dlebag. Then, with the hide spread out on the grass to protect the meat, they sawed the hindquarters from the carcass, then separated them. Ward instructed Eric to cut the legs off below the knee using the saw. Using a combination of saw and knife, Ward cut a saddle out of the back and ribs. Finally, they sliced away the front shoulder, and Eric marveled at how an appendage could support such weight without having a socket.

They slipped the quarters and meat into muslin game bags that

Lorraine had made from old sheets. Ward stacked up the parts on the hide, appraising them for size and weight, shuffling the stacks around, hefting them, muttering calculations.

Then he carefully wiped his tools off with his handkerchief. He silently walked to the edge of the clearing, stretching his back as he went, and pulled at a dead pine branch. It cracked like a rifle shot when it broke. Ward snapped the branch in half and walked back, tapping the piece of wood on his thigh. At the juniper bush where the elk had fallen, he stopped and cut a half-dozen sprigs, then jammed the stick into the ground with an exhalation of breath and stomped on it with his heel.

"Bring me the old girl's head, would you, Eric?"

Eric gingerly picked up the severed head by the ears and walked over to where Ward stood.

"As you probably know, since I suspect you've read up on elk hunting, these critters have a set of ivory teeth amongst their upper canines. Ordinarily, this is when we cut them out. But I say we leave them. Any opinions?"

What opinion could he possibly have on whether or not to extract teeth? It sounded like a grisly ritual. But he knew Ward was trying to say something.

"Beats genuflecting in the nave, I guess."

"My thoughts, too. Set her down over that stick."

"Over it? You mean right on top?" The idea struck Eric as barbaric. "Head on a pike pole," he said. "What sort of offering is that?"

Ward, who was weaving the juniper sprigs together, tucking the branches into each other said, "It's more of a memorial."

Eric almost said Oh Christ, then didn't. He eased the head down over the stick, adjusting it so the head wouldn't lean this way or that. Then he poked the tongue, still warm, back into the mouth.

Ward silently continued to manipulate the juniper branches until they formed a crown. Using his knife, he trimmed off a few errant twigs, then carefully placed the crown on the cow's head, slipping it down on the outside of her ears.

They stood before the head, not knowing quite what to say, then deciding that saying nothing was probably best. The moment was not made for speech. Ward moved first, turning towards the horses, singing to himself, an old Youngbloods' song.

THEY FILLED the panniers with Ward adjusting for weight. Bullet's panniers carried the two hindquarters and the saddle of elk. LJ, who objected to the smell, carried the two front quarters and the rolled-up hide. Ward strung the two horses together then gave the rope to Eric. "Why don't you lead?"

A drizzle trickled through the trees in gray afternoon light. The occasional snowflake landed on the ground.

They walked in silence. Eric felt so spent for once he wished he were riding. A vacant feeling again pervaded him, a void that took away flesh and bones. He saw himself as an empty vessel, ghostly, with two legs walking in front of a solid flea-bitten gray horse through October weather. The sensation had enormous black potential; but it also had a strangely comforting aura. The emptiness demanded nothing of him and felt clean and almost pure. He shivered, knowing that his mind had never been so clear, not even as a child. He could not recall a time when he hadn't packed his brain with visions of greatness. Events of the morning had blown open his circuitry with hallucinogenic power and let him take in the attendant strength of just *this* day.

Ward looked up at the sky.

"Some of those raindrops are starting to float. I say we head home first thing tomorrow morning. Getting the trailer off the mountain in snow can be a chore. What do you think?"

"What about your elk?"

"Only one elk needs to be shot this year."

"You sure?"

"Positive. We've still got some of last year's elk and mule deer in the freezer."

They walked through a small creek, reduced to no more than a trickle, then up a steep embankment on the other side. At the top, Ward checked the panniers and took over the lead.

"Lorraine tells me you've been selling songs to Billy Madden. True?"

"Few years back."

"How many did you sell?"

"Just to Madden or altogether?"

Ward cinched down a strap then took the lead rope. They continued walking, Eric in the lead.

"Altogether."

"I never counted. Over twenty-five, probably closer to thirty-five. They were goofy songs, though, and the royalty business dried up before long."

Ward twirled the spare footage of the lead rope around in his hand. "How much do you suppose other people have made off your songs?"

"A lot."

"And you don't own a house? How goofy is that?" said Ward.

"I know," said Eric, "and I owned a few palatial houses in my day. Now I'm down to a vehicle, my guitars, piano, amps, some furniture, and books. That's it."

"You're miles ahead, believe me, Eric. What was Bunyan's aphorism? You remember that? Something like 'A man there was, tho' some did count him mad. The more he cast away, the more he had.' That sound right?'"

"You're asking the wrong person. I've never been much of a success at ascetic aspirations. Always wanted more. Honestly. I never went for the simple-is-better line of reasoning. The joy I received out of playing a six-thousand-dollar custom-made guitar far exceeded the pleasure I got from sticking with a plain-old Strat. Nothing wrong with a Stratocaster. I own four. Or did. When I was on that commune in Mendocino, I'd work on that old John Deere, pretending I was working on a Mercedes, all the while running those Ram Dass witticisms through my head, you know: 'Be here now.'

'Be present.' 'Don't project.' Finally, I gave up. What's the use, I told myself. You want what you want."

They were out of the trees. A dusting of snow began sticking to the ground.

"Cabin's not a half a mile from here," said Ward, looking around. "How are your feet?"

Eric had forgotten about his feet.

"Getting wet and they do hurt. I don't know, Ward. Maybe you're right. Maybe I should have stuck with fixing tractors in the Coast Range."

"You never struck me as the commune-dwelling type, Eric. If you spent the whole time dreaming about being someplace else, then you didn't belong there."

"Gets to be a goddamn permanent mindset, though. Been that way ever I was a kid craving to get out of Valentine. Never satisfied. Escape mechanism, etcetera. Didn't you ever do that?"

Ward scoffed but didn't stop walking. "Don't forget who I was, Lindsay. The eldest male, the scion, of a founding California family. A maximum security prison could not have higher walls. Why do you think I was at Berkeley studying the wisdom of the ancients? Digging myself an escape route."

"I always envied your life."

Ward shook his head and half-melted flakes spun off his hat.

"And I yours."

The admission stunned Eric.

"You did? Why the hell would someone in your position envy a scrawny opportunistic kid from the Sand Hills?"

"You had it all, Lindsay. Talent and unvarnished ambition. An adjustable future. Mine was scripted from birth. And the simplicity of it. That's what I loved about Gwen. She was my Desdemona, my Nebraska girl with no trust fund and no father who expected you to be president of the goddamn United States."

"Yeah, but you never met our mother."

"Ah, but that was one thing we had in common: autocratic

puppet-master mothers. That became clear as day when we shared that house at Berkeley. I remember those phone calls that would send you sideways. Gwen and I talked about that. Your mother wrote me letters, you know."

"My mother?"

"A half-dozen at least. Notes of pure rage. Don't blame her."

"Did you ever write back?"

Ward let out a sigh. "No. In fact, I never knew she wrote the letters until much later. My mother hid them from me. I only found them after she'd died. She covered me like a wet blanket. Spared me from taking responsibility for my actions. After I shot Gwen, she ran my life for half a dozen years."

After I shot Gwen.

"But it's never too late," Ward added.

"Late for what?"

"To get on that bronc and hold on and learn to love it. Never too late."

"That's what Lorraine said when I told her I wasn't saved. Never too late," Eric said.

"Well, it's not. How is your mother, by the way?"

"Miserable, as usual. She's just as unhappy with dementia as she was clear-headed."

———

WARD MUSTERED enough gumption to heat a bucket of water on the kitchen stove. They took off their shirts and with dishwashing soap silently scrubbed the elk blood off their hands and arms, their skin stinging from the nicks and cuts. Eric saw Ward's eyes quickly run over his body with concern in his eyes.

"I'm a little underweight, aren't I?"

"You look one of those cows in Russell's painting, 'Waiting for a Chinook.' You ever see that?"

"Yeah, in one of Gwen's art books."

Ward grinned but the concern never left his eyes.

Eric pulled off the medicine pouch and handed it to him, but

Ward shook his head. "Why don't you wear that until we get back to the house? It seems like it does you good."

Eric immediately fell asleep when he slid down into his sleeping bag. He woke up two hours later, knee pounding, his clean T-shirt soaked, the medicine pouch wrapped up around his neck. He sat up and was immediately cold. The temperature had dropped dramatically since they'd sunk down into their beds, so tired they barely had the energy to eat a bowl of Lorraine's chili.

Eric got up and restoked the fading bed of coals. He shook out two ibuprofen and swallowed them with cold water straight from the pump. He stood beside the stove and looked at the lump of Ward in his bed. Unlike previous nights, Ward had not moved much, or Eric didn't think he had. Was he all right? Was that the way the deal worked? The man he wanted dead manages to live, yet dies by the whims of fate? Eric crept across the cold floor and peered at Ward's shape. It rose and fell in a slow rhythm.

Eric scuttled back to the stove, opened the door and stared at the fire. How many times had he turned away? How many times had he retreated from participation on the grounds that it was not worth his time or that it would invariably have sour results? How many times had he turned from his first wife, Candice? She wanted children from the day they were married. She even tricked him once, saying she forgot to take the pill for a few weeks. He didn't even know she was pregnant until she miscarried. Now she and her husband had four girls. How often had he turned from Alyson, who ached for his approval and a man who was demonstratively affectionate?

By the light of the open stove door, he rummaged in his duffle until he found his long underwear tops and bottoms. He stripped off his damp T-shirt, still smelling the elk's musty scent on his skin and the moisture of the pouch. A shivering, dank chill ran through his upper body, but he instantly regained warmth after donning the long underwear and a fleece jacket. He felt as if he were plugged in to electric current.

He went to the window. Stars were out, and yet it looked like it was still snowing. How could one see the heavens and snowflakes at the same time? Wasn't it always either/or? The urge to be out in starlight and snow seized him, immediately followed by a list of reasons why he should not indulge this notion. He found his bivy sack, pad, and polar fleece hat. He grabbed his sleeping bag and, tugging on his fleece boots, stepped out into the cold.

A half-open sky, the marquee of stars unobstructed, competed with a bank of clouds dropping fat, white flakes. Beneath a pine where the snow barely hid the needles, he flopped down his gear and arranged himself accordingly, using his boots as a pillow. Sliding down in the bag and bivy sack, he felt himself more insect than human, as if he were entering a chrysalis.

Through the branches, the celestial theater scuttled across the sky on a slow-moving conveyor belt. For the first time in his life, he gave himself permission to really look at the Milky Way. No angry soliloquies gained the stage; no voices in his head tried to take over; no compressor blew in tension, like fluffy, loose insulation being forced into the airspace of an attic; no worry about the potential cold or servicing debt or mother's shortcomings or avenging or solving anything.

He saw himself for what he was—a man, nearly a half-century old, as Graham would say, alternatively getting his face bathed in million-year-old starlight filtered through a thin veil of pine boughs then, the next minute, seeing black clouds and feeling snowflakes melt on his cheeks.

He had no visions and wouldn't have trusted one if he had. He slept.

A door slammed. Eric woke and lifted his head. Ward stood on the porch, looking at him. He waved. Eric waved back. He was ready for anything.

———

WARD STOOD before the stove in boot liners, jacket, and long underwear, groaning, muttering about the perils of old age, and tossed a dozen sticks of pine kindling onto the coals. He opened up the draft on the stove and, after a minute's delay, there was a whoosh as the kindling burst into flame, roaring. Ward surprised Eric by pulling out an ancient espresso maker from a kitchen cabinet, explaining it was a tradition in camp to have serious coffee the morning after someone got an elk.

While waiting for the water to boil, Ward pulled on pants and a pair of boots and went to feed the horses; Eric tossed more wood onto the fire. The cabin filled with the smell of burning pine resin and strong coffee. Eric wondered if a more divine combination of odors ever existed.

Ward returned carrying a ziplock bag of elk meat. "If I sautéed some backstrap in olive oil and fried up a few eggs on the side, would you eat it? Or are you going to continue your starvation diet?"

The smell of the espresso had created good stirrings in his stomach. For the first time in what seemed weeks, Eric actually felt the pang of hunger.

"I guess I could eat some."

The smell of sautéed elk joined the odors of coffee and pine smoke. They ate slowly, in silence, sopping up the egg yolk and juice from the elk backstrap with thick slabs of Lorraine's homemade bread, which Ward toasted on the stovetop. Eric could not remember when a meal felt so satisfying. The sensation eased the worry lingering in the back of his mind about why he was not hungry.

He got up to go outside for a smoke and Ward waved him back down to his chair. "Go ahead. Smoke. Place needs fumigating."

As they packed, Eric's burning legs and thighs forced him to concentrate in order to keep up with Ward, who seemed able to put his weariness aside. Both horses had thrown shoes and Ward quietly fumed about his lack of observation in not noticing this the day before. Eric drew a five-gallon bucket of water from the pump and covered it, leaving it for the next time Ward used the cabin. They loaded the horses and elk meat last, setting the meat in the tack room. LJ, smelling the elk, thrashed around in the trailer banging the sides until Ward told him to quit.

After staggering under the weight of the elk quarters, Eric felt lightheaded. A sudden pain shot up his back and chest and he began to cough. He leaned against the trailer for support. Warm phlegm moved to the top of his throat and he spat. There, in tracks indented in clean snow, were little speckles of blood, perfectly round, bubbled-filled, and brilliant against the white.

Ward, staring at the blood, readjusted his hat and cleared his throat. He said slowly, "You might want to see somebody about that when you get back to L.A., Lindsay."

Eric nodded. "I haven't felt too well for a while."

About halfway down the mountain, Ward brought the truck and trailer to a dead stop at a hairpin turn so they both could look up at a draw where the scarlet chokecherry leaves ran so thick it looked like the blood Eric had recently spat on the snow.

"Goddamn, will you look at that?" said Ward. "Isn't that magnificent?"

"You've gotten pretty liberal with the goddamns in the last day or so. What's Lorraine going to say?"

"Tweak my ear."

"Seriously."

"I am serious. I use the Lord's name in vain and she reaches out and twists my ear like I'm an errant schoolboy. Not always, but when I do it in front of the boys, she always does something to let me know she doesn't like it one bit."

"Pardon me for prying, Fall, but how do you two reconcile your approaches to the world?"

Ward shrugged as if to acknowledge that they did have their differences. "We are alike in strange ways," said Ward. "She has had trouble, like me. We are both outcasts of a sort: her from her colony and me from my old California world."

He paused. "We have our sore spots, mostly over-protection and exposure. She grew up in an ultra-sheltered environment. No television. No radio unless it was a weather station. No movies. Now she wants to shield the boys in the same manner. I agree in principle, selective information, but it can lead to a warped and naïve take on things. Ptolemaic, in fact. You and your world at the center of the universe. New ideas and events are so much of a shock you can't take them in, can't process them, can't live with them. You build not only walls but glass bubbles."

Ward checked on the trailer with his side mirror. "Funny thing. That's a way Lorraine and I are alike. We both grew up in bubbles. If there is one thing I can do, it's build edifices with one-way glass. I can see out but no one can see in. The problem is my view out is just as limited as the view in. When I bailed from the University of Chicago, my doctoral thesis in tatters, I took refuge at the Ladderback. Thought if I could just stay there, reading and raising Herefords, everything would be okay."

"Was it?"

"Sure. For a while, but it wasn't. Like you, I wanted to be someplace else, mostly outside of my own skin. I thought I'd die when the Ladderback was sold, per order of the bankruptcy court, but then I realized I was relieved. I'd been given a shot at creating my own world."

He paused. "Besides, with me and Lorraine, what's to reconcile, really?"

"Well," said Eric, "any man who can read Heidegger and actually understand the obtuse SOB has a pretty firm grasp of abstractions. Lorraine strikes me as having a fairly literal outlook on the world, including a reading of scripture. I'm just impressed that you two can make it work."

Ward took his eyes off the road and gave him a nod of appreciation, like Eric had finally said something that affirmed an important choice in his life.

"Lorraine's not like us, Lindsay. She's not scared of getting screwed or being a fool. I am. Scared of being duped. Scared of being labeled naïve and gullible. Personally, I'm tired of it. If Lorraine's taught me anything it's that cranial capacity has little to do with contentment. It's a sickness, a deep sickness, that people believe that they've got to think complicated in order to think smart."

Yeah, thought Eric. In fact, most of his life, he had been known as the person who supplied answers and solutions to musical problems, a station or outlook with little tolerance for naiveté or simplistic thinking. Sophistication and aesthetics had been his bywords.

"I guess I've been vigilant ever since my second-grade teacher posited that the sun orbited the earth," Eric said. "Gwen and I knew she was wrong and couldn't imagine someone in that position of authority saying such a wacko thing. I was always questioning."

"Me, too," said Ward, steering the truck and trailer around a tree brought down by the weight of new snow. "But with Lorraine, that sort of vigilance would destroy her whole faith. Who would want to destroy a person's faith, Eric? Some sort of belief beats the hell out of a syllogism or tending a reductionist's zoo."

"I don't believe I've ever had the pleasure of visiting such an establishment."

"Sure you have. Pavlov's dog, Lorenz's geese, Skinner's rats."

"I see. But you, yourself, can't share this faith?"

"I try, Eric. But I've got to work for it. After I killed Gwen, I had to work for everything, every shred of happiness that came my way. Hell, I had to work for it before the accident. I've been down in the belly of the whale."

I killed Gwen.

They went a long time in silence. When they drove past Yellow Legs's house, just one dog, a hound of mixed lineage, sat in the driveway and silently watched them go by. Eric was further rattled to hear himself say, "I felt his presence."

"Whose?"

"Yellow Legs."

"The hell you say."

"I don't know, it's odd," said Eric. "When you told me about

Yellow Legs being a tracker of the first order, it sort of jarred my plans. It introduced an element of reality, it laid open all the grimness my plan entailed. The first domino of my fantasy fell. The last being, of course, the realization that you'd set this whole thing up. That was awful clever, Fall."

Eric looked at Ward, feeling apprehensive. Ward said nothing for a couple minutes. Just as Eric concluded that Ward wasn't going to respond at all, he said, "Cleverness had nothing to do with it. It was desperation. Sheer bottom-of-the-barrel desperation."

Ward reached up and scratched the growth on his face. "I don't know, Lindsay. I'm feeling pretty overwhelmed, like I've just been through a battle in which I assumed I would die, like those soldiers in the Civil War who wrote their own obituaries before the first shot was fired. When you walk out the other side, free of bullet holes, the universe looks different. It looks…" Ward hesitated, grinned, then snorted, "…big. How about you?"

"Fall, I've got a space around my brain about the size of a national park in which all sorts of goblins and their kin are dancing around."

"My. That's pretty colorful, not to mention dramatic."

"Yeah, but it's not bothering me too much. But it definitely feels weird, very fucking weird. You know, Fall, I'll be fifty pretty soon. Thus far, all I've been able to conclude from this strange chapter in my life is that I better get my ass in gear. I've got a lot of catching up to do. I'm not sure what I'm supposed to catch. Things might not turn out the way I thought they would."

Ward shook his head in wonder, the way Eric's father had done when looking at a big paycheck. He reached over and rubbed the dust off the piece of paper that read SURRENDER IS NOT SLAVERY.

"Lorraine wrote that. She didn't ask if she could put it there. She just did it. All you can do is hope that faith comes. And it comes to Lorraine like water from a mountain spring. Grace. More than grace. Her faith is as real as trees, tangible as a smooth ash handle of an old hay rake."

Eric looked out the window and watched the shadow of the truck and trailer shrink and expand on the new snow as they drove over rolling hills. He didn't know what to say to such a lyric explanation. Faith as a gift? My whole life has the aura of swindle, he thought.

Suddenly he felt very tired and slipped down in the seat, letting the diesel's drone lull him. That tour with Brooks reminded him that there was no sleeping aid like the basso of a diesel.

———

WARD DIDN'T make it to the shower until late. His skin crawled with old sweat but an unending series of tasks kept him from cleaning up.

After the last bit of camp gear had been cleaned and stowed, Eric having retired to the office, the boys in bed, and after the last telling of the story of how Eric got his elk and the fib of how he'd been whacked in the face by a pine branch when horseback, Ward wearily peeled off this clothes, the small bathroom filling with the odors of a body that thought, just yesterday, it was going to die. He expected Lorraine to slip into the bathroom at any moment. She liked to make love the night he came back from camp, liked to hold him while he still emanated sweat, body odor, elk musk, and blood. She insisted that his genitals be clean, however, and made him stand in the bathtub while she soaped him up with a washcloth.

But tonight she did not come. Ward tried, while sticking his hand in the shower to feel the temperature, to calculate her ovulation cycle in his head. It should be a good time to couple up, but he never, even in his randiest moments, questioned her judgment concerning fertility. Besides, he had more to wash off than dirt but wasn't sure soap would clean all the sorrow from under his skin. The hot water made him suck in his breath and came close to scalding him, but he didn't add any cold.

He closed his eyes and began to scrub. The vision of Eric's blood-speckled spit coloring the snow rose before him. How long did he have to live? Not long, probably. What was going through

Eric's head? Yet the poor bastard actually looked happy, the happiest he'd ever seen him.

Ward began at his toes and with a long-handled brush, scrubbed his skin until it burned and tingled. The rush of blood made him glow and lulled him into a state of mild euphoria, as if his whole body was reveling in the news that it had the freedom to grow a new layer of skin. He distrusted such sensations as they almost always involved a descent that held him captive long after any feeling of pleasure had disappeared.

As the water poured down on his head, he recalled the first real attempt to deal with the death of Gwen. He'd taken a year abroad from Berkeley to study at Heidelberg. At Christmas, he fled that icy city for Greece and met his brother on the island of Patmos. There, they lounged on the beach, flirted with Swedish girls, and stared up at the monastery built to honor the revelations of Saint John. The edifice towered above the white puzzle of houses. Ward wondered how such a monolith could possibly honor the vivid, hallucinatory liquid visions of John. "The word became flesh." Not even a madman like William Blake could make such a leap.

But one night, as Ward washed the sea salt off his body in a lukewarm shower, he saw how he'd built such a citadel around Gwen's death. He'd cemented it with brick and mortar. But whereas the monastery was built to keep the revelation alive, his inner citadel was constructed to keep anything from examining her death. He went to a *taverna* and drank himself sick on *retsina*.

In the shower, he could still taste the piney wine in his mouth and felt bile inching up his esophagus. Yet in the shower in Hake's Fork, he saw that monastery in Patmos crumble, brick by brick. It wasn't the church and chapel that fell, but the huge wall and battlements around the buildings that buckled as if shaken by earthquake, dust rising.

He bent over in the shower and vomited. When he stood up, he felt hugely relieved and almost in a trance. He barely heard the shower door slide open. Lorraine stood there in her bra and panties.

"Ward? Are you all right? My word, you're pink as a hot dog."

He found himself momentarily without reply. Finally he blurted, "Just trying to get clean."

She momentarily closed the door, undressed fully, then got in the shower with him, not the slightest bit concerned that she was stepping in vomit. She put her arms around him. He rested his chin on the top of her head. She looked up at him, her eyes searching, wanting answers.

"Something happened up there, didn't it? I could see it in your eyes, including this one," she said, touching the lid of his swollen eye. "A pine branch didn't do this, did it?"

"No, and yes something happened."

She squeezed him around the chest, pressing herself into him. "Oh, I prayed to God it would. The nights you were gone, my knees practically wore holes in that bedroom carpet; I prayed with all my might. Did you talk about what happened with Gwen?"

"Yes."

"Can you tell me about it?"

He told her about the canyon incident. He felt her take a sharp intake of breath when he described himself walking up the hill to await Eric's bullet. Then her body shook as she wept, but she kept silent but for little gasps of breath. Finally she said in a half-moan, "Oh, Ward, my Ward. And you're okay?"

"I don't know what I feel, really. Relieved. I don't know what it all means."

She sighed and hugged him tighter. "Well, that's a first. Mr. Know-it-all can't explain something."

Then she kissed him on the chest.

"It's going to take me a while to sort this out, Lorraine."

"Of course it will. But you've just walked out of the valley of the shadow of death, Ward."

"Funny. I mentioned Bunyan to Eric just yesterday. The quote about having less means having more. Didn't Christian encounter a hell of a lot more woes after he managed to survive the valley?"

"Vanity Fair," said Lorraine, spitting out some water. "But you're good at resisting the temptation. That's not your struggle, Ward. You know that."

She squeezed him again. "You are such a strange man. And I love you so for it. You set yourself up to a standard you can't possibly meet. Somewhere along the path we're going to trip. All of us do. All these years you've told yourself you couldn't live, live with dignity, I mean, after what happened with Gwen. What sort of life is that, Ward?"

She looked up at him.

"That's your struggle: trying to live a life when you don't think you have a right to live. Didn't you shed yourself of that burden? That's what I mean about walking out of the valley of the shadow of death."

She reached up and took the back of his neck and put his head directly under the shower's stream. And then the water in the shower turned cold, bracing to skin, but his inner core remained warm.

CHAPTER 8

FLYING HOME, ERIC FELT exhausted and clean, as if he'd been in a steam bath that expunged his brain. No pressure in his head. No concentric circles of squabbling and dread. His clothes, washed in hard Hake's Fork water, had a new feel. He put a blanket over his head and slept.

He awoke thinking he heard one of the movements from *Dreams of the Whippoorwill* over the airplane's PA system. He almost started humming it out loud; but another movement faded in, overdubbing itself on the first. Then they came in a flood, as if he were changing stations on the radio and all stations were playing his songs. It was his voice and with guitar, not piano, in the background. It sounded good.

The 911 engine crooned to him in a new tone on the way home from the airport. He stopped at his favorite tobacconist to stock up, reminding himself that whatever was down in his lungs, tobacco wouldn't help matters, then bought a quart of orange juice, three bottles of mineral water, and two sets of extra-light guitar strings.

Then he bought a portable Sony DAT audio recorder.

Los Angeles had acquired a lizard skin, rough and scaly. He realized he'd been putting up with the hardness for twenty years now, fighting it every day, yet telling himself it was just part of life and he'd better learn to like it. He saw that he did not like it or dislike it, but he knew it was a place that could not hold him much longer.

But then where would he live? Before he had left for Hake's Fork, he'd noticed Mr. Chou no longer was taking his morning walk. A series of unfamiliar cars came and went from his landlord's house. Maybe it was silly to worry about such things with him coughing up blood.

He did not bother to unpack. He hung blankets over the windows and picked through his rack of guitar cases. He pulled out a battered black case and set it on the floor. He opened it and stared at the guitar, much in the same way Ward had stared at his rifle.

It was a 1938 Martin D-28 herringbone, his father's prized guitar, way too much instrument for a man more inclined towards fiddles and piano. He'd bought it at a pawn shop in Omaha during World War II.

It looked practically new. About ten years back, Eric had the guitar restored. True to his generous nature, his father had loaned the guitar out to trusted—and some not-so-trusted—musicians. It was worn, with a large amount of pickwear on the treble side of the first string. Over decades dings and nicks had crept into the surface. The dull finish on the back of the neck revealed his father's inclination to play in the first position. It badly needed a new bridge and neck reset.

When the luthier returned the guitar, Eric rarely played it and instead treated it like a museum piece, which he knew was silly. It had a glorious bass response. It sounded like a cello and possessed the warmth and depth of a classical guitar; yet it could snarl and whine the blues like no other acoustic instrument he'd ever played.

Those songs he'd heard in his head on the airplane, most of them written on the Rhodes, had this guitar playing in the background—deep, resonant with crisp clear high end, especially when played with extra-light strings.

An urgency bordering on compulsion drove him. He transposed *Dreams of the Whippoorwill* from piano to guitar and recorded until his fingers numbed, then bled. He stopped for a day, ate his first real meal, then began to edit and re-record. A new level of exhaustion fell over him. Still he couldn't sleep. He lay on the bed for hours, unable to doze, even as ocean light crept into his windows. Finally he took a Halcion. He awoke with *Dreams of the Whippoorwill* still in his head.

He put just two songs on a cassette then went to find Graham. They had not talked for months, the longest period of silence Eric could remember. He dropped off the tape at his downtown office, leaving it with a secretary.

Graham didn't call that day, nor the following day, nor the day after that. Eric felt his energy and hope wane and eventually curdle. He felt a childish rejection. And the whole project seemed silly.

The cars at Mr. Chou's house belonged to nurses or living assistants, Eric surmised. Mr. Chou did not come out onto the back porch to smoke.

A jingle producer actually took the time to drive to his house and asked to come in and do an overdub. Eric obliged. On the way home, his cell rang. When he answered, *Dreams of the Whippoorwill* hissed and wavered through the air. He wondered if he was being revisited by those auditory hallucinations he'd heard on the plane. Then came Graham's voice, arched and high in excitement.

"Lindsay?"

"Yes? Graham!"

"I believe your train has arrived."

"What's that mean?"

Graham's word tumbled out. "That means I've been listening to your tape for two days. I've got it in the deck right now. Can't seem to get it out of my head. Where the bloody hell did you come up with this stuff? Don't think I've ever heard anything quite like this, certainly not from you. It's so distilled with both tension and sweetness. Very clever melodic motif. You've been working on these for a while, haven't you?"

"Yes.

"I knew it. Record them in your living room?"

"Bedroom."

"Why didn't you come down to the crypt? How many tracks did you lay down?

"Couple dozen."

"Can I hear them?"

"Some are just sketches, really, Graham. Pretty rough. Not worth a listen."

"Let me be the judge of that. Let's give them a spin, eh?"

"Sure. When?"

"Today."

"Today?

"The crypt in, say, three hours. Around two-thirty."

"Sure."

"Right. Bring me everything you've got. Don't bloody hold out on me now."

Everything. Graham would squawk when he found out how much material he had.

"Okay."

"Sheet music, too."

"Okay."

"Brilliant. See you at two-thirty."

Then he hung up.

The crypt was a studio in Graham's basement, a room where he hid to listen to final takes. The studio incorporated half the basement floor space. Thousands of CDs and records lined the shelves. The room had three pianos, including a baby grand, and a late-model Yamaha electric that stood behind Graham's desk, which was piled high with papers. Graham sat behind the stacks, surrounded by a halo of smoke. He smoked, like Eric's father, Pall Mall straights. Eric loved that he, like himself, made no apologies for his habit. Graham looked up from a score and took off his reading glasses. He seemed genuinely glad to see him.

He rose and put out his hand. "Ah. Lindsay. Sit down. Tea?"

"No. Thanks."

Graham sat back down. "Well, I'm going to make myself a cup."

Graham pushed his chair back as if to get a bigger view of Eric, but offered no opinion.

He turned on the electric kettle he kept on the counter, then packed a tea ball with leaves from a tin.

"You're not in jail."

"I took a few steps to prevent such an occurrence."

"Including a tour with Brooks, I hear. How did it go?"

Eric shrugged. "Okay. Not as bad as I thought."

"What have you been doing since the tour ended? Working on this project?" He reached across the desk, making impatient motions with hands.

Eric handed him a folder of sheet music and paused. How could you possibly explain what had happened to him? He couldn't.

"I took care of some old business."

Graham appraised him more carefully and nodded his head. Eric felt his eyes run over him, like Ward's eyes had done in elk camp, and wondered if Graham would inquire further.

"You look different."

"I do? How?"

"Don't know. Couldn't say, really. You've somehow managed to get some sun. You look more relaxed. Still too bleeding thin."

Graham nodded again and paused long enough to light another cigarette. "Whatever you've been up to, I'd say keep doing it." He tapped the song folder, then opened it up. When he put on his glasses, Graham immediately looked up. "This is all for the piano?"

"Originally it was. But somehow I started hearing these songs being played on the D-28. So, I started transposing. But for you I brought down the keyboard sheet music."

"Well now," said Graham approvingly, and began leafing through the material. "Ah," he murmured after about a minute. Then silence followed by a bit of humming.

Graham was silent long enough for the ash on his cigarette to drop off, his breathing raspy and heavy. Occasionally there'd be a sigh of pleasure.

Finally, he said, "This I've got to try," and rolled his chair over to the Yamaha electric. "This is on the tape, right? Second song or movement or whatever you call them?"

Eric nodded, apprehensive about hearing someone else play *Dreams of the Whippoorwill*.

Graham played about ten bars, slowly, feeling his way into the piece, then stopped, uttering more monosyllabic utterances of approval. Then he hesitated and Eric saw the same reluctance he saw in his father when he played a piece of new music. Even the best are unsure, he said to himself, but still they press on. Graham went back and repeated the last four bars, this time holding the sustain pedal all the way down, the way it was supposed to be played.

"Ah, lovely. This is one of those pieces that's easy to play but nearly impossible to master, isn't it? Tension is what it has; very sophisticated yet it's straightforward as a nursery rhyme. When did you write this?"

"Been working on it for years, I suppose."

"Sneaky bastard, you."

Graham leaned back in his chair, staring at him, then back at the music. He flipped the page. "No double bar?"

"No, it's not really a coda. They're all connected."

"I see. What do you call these compositions?"

"Dreams of the Whippoorwill."

"I like that," Graham glanced down, shuffling the sheets around. "Very fitting."

He put the music down. The kettle whistled, and Graham made himself a cup of tea. He scooted his chair back to his desk, holding his cup. "What's your schedule look like?"

"When?"

"Now."

"Empty."

"So is mine. Had a major cancellation this morning. Rehab for lead vocalist. Let's cut a CD."

"You really have time?"

"I have the time, Eric. Shall we do it? Don't think too hard, please."

"Yes."

"Brilliant. That's the answer I wanted to hear. Let's get some paperwork out of the way, shall we? And, we'll have to eventually find a label, of course," Graham began shuffling papers on his desk. "An agent would help. You have ever stooped to having one?"

"My dealings with agents did not have harmonious endings, Graham. You know that. We can make a recording but could you get me a contract?"

Graham bobbed his tea ball in his cup, pulled hard on his cigarette, and blew out the smoke through his nose like a dragon. He sighed again in mild exasperation.

"I've never known a sod so picky about how people shovel the shit that he won't shovel himself. Anyone you know have a great and abiding affection for agents? Tell me that? They're knee-deep in the sewer so you don't have to be. But...."

He took the tea ball out of the cup, placing on the saucer. "I, like everyone else in your life, will make an exception because you're so damn good. But you know that. Now this," he waved the music around like a baton. "Where the hell was I when God handed out the bloody talent? Shoveling coke in a Birmingham mill, that's where. It's going to be a bit of a tough sell, music like this is. I can get you a contract, I think. Give me a few days. How much time do you have?"

Eric thought about those red speckles on the snow and thought again that he really should go see a physician. "Not much."

"Good. Some music gets lost if you dawdle."

Graham squinted his eyes, as if what he was going to say personally pained him. "No one will front you productions costs, though. Including me. You have to cover those."

"How much would that be?"

"Depends. It might be as much as twenty-five grand, possibly more."

"That's doable."

"Does doable involve loan sharks or handguns?"

"No."

"Promise?"

"I promise."

"Excellent."

"Any preference on a studio? Want to do it here?"

"Do you know of any place that still uses one of those older thirty-two-track analogues?"

Graham began scribbling on a notepad. "Think so. Anything else?"

"Musicians," said Eric.

"You need any?" asked Graham, surprised, glancing up from his notes. "Can you afford them? What couldn't you play?"

"It's not a matter of ability. It's a matter of feel," said Eric, thinking out loud.

"Tell me more."

"Some of these songs require different tones, colors, really, colors I think would be very difficult for me to produce. I think I want to stick to the guitar."

"Dear God. Thought I'd never see this day."

"Will you play keyboards?"

"Me?"

"Why not?"

"Because I'm fucking ancient and haven't recorded—except in emergencies—for years."

"But you still practice?"

"Yes."

"Daily?"

"Most days, yes."

"So you'll do keyboards? Union scale."

"Oh, sod off. I'll count this as a freebee."

"Then I need a female vocalist. I don't know who I want, Graham, I just know the sound that's in my head."

"And what's that sound?"

"I want the sound of Lorraine Fall singing in her living room," he said. "In her trailer."

Graham folded his hands patiently. "And who, pray tell, is Lorraine Fall? Have I heard her before?"

Eric sat up with the vision of Lorraine Fall in an L.A. studio. "No, but you will. It will take a couple days to get her here."

Graham raised his eyes. "Okay. You're picking the musicians. Bass player?"

"Yes. Someone with a subtle touch. And a violinist on standby."

"A violinist?" Graham stopped taking notes and stared at him, squinting from the smoke, cigarette motionless in his mouth. "Didn't you once play a terrific fiddle part on Dixie Clark's CD?"

Eric nodded.

"You act like you've been thinking about this for a while."

"All my life."

"Right. Next time, just tell me sooner, okay?"

———

ABOUT SELLING something you think can't ever being sold: it's actually not a wrenching moment of anguish, but, when you're ready, it's an act as easy as giving away a bucket of rainwater. It only took Eric one phone call to sell the D-28. "You can have it the day I finish this recording," he told the buyer, "but I need half the money now." The idea came to him, crashing like a wave, as he drove back from meeting with Graham. The thought shocked him at first. His first response was to come up with an immediate list of alternatives: go to the bank, sell the 911 instead, wholesale all the other guitars. No. Just sell the D-28.

———

WARD LAY in bed, reading, listening to Lorraine's chatter on the telephone. He was pretty sure she was talking with Eric Lindsay.

When the conversation stopped, she came into the bedroom, undoing her hair, smiling, looking pleased with herself.

"That was Eric."

"So I gathered. How's he doing?"

She picked up a brush. "He's making a CD."

"Hasn't he done that before?

"Not of his own music." She started to brush her hair. "He wants me to fly to L.A. and sing vocals on it."

Ward put down his book on the quilt.

"Seriously?"

"Uh-huh. Can you believe that?"

"When?"

"Next week."

"What did you say?"

"Well, I told him I wouldn't sing any songs about sex or drinking or drugs."

"I guess you won't be singing much, will you?"

Lorraine went to the mirror and continued brushing. "He said some of the songs didn't even have words. He needed my voice as background vocals."

Ward waited.

"I told him I'd come. He wants you to come, too. I said we would. Is that okay?"

So typical of Lorraine, thought Ward. Does what she pleases, then asks permission.

"What about the kids?"

"I was thinking about getting my sister and cousin Dolores from the colony to come stay here. They're always looking for ways to make money."

"You're finally going to get that expensive airplane ride."

Years ago when thinking about buying the MK, Ward had hired a single-engine Cessna to fly over the ranch. He had taken Lorraine with him. It was their third date. It was the first and only time she had flown in a plane.

"Eric said he'd pay for it, too. Besides, I've ridden in an airplane before."

"I mean one that fits more than two people. Well, how about that. My wife the recording star."

"Oh, stop it."

"He really wants me to come?"

"Of course. *I* want you to come. I'm not going to the big city by myself."

"Did he mention anything about his health?"

"No. Why should he? What's the matter?"

"He's pretty sick, I think."

She tilted her head and brushed her hair in long strokes, but her eyes, through the reflection, were on Ward. "Really? What kind of sick? Besides being as skinny as one of those poor reservation dogs."

"He was coughing blood up in the mountains."

She stopped the comb mid-stroke and turned to Ward. "What? He was? Why didn't you say anything before?"

"I'm not sure Eric wanted his health status known to the general public. And I don't know for certain the nature of the problem."

"Well, I'll get it out of him. I hope he's okay."

———

THEY RECORDED for three days. On the afternoon of the third day, Eric and Lorraine attempted harmony voice-overs on a track. Eric's part had a very narrow range of notes—just five—all within his reach, but he had to be absolutely focused. Into the third bar, his voice faltered and he held up his hand to stop the band. Lorraine glanced at him in worry. His chest felt tight again, like it did on the day of the Berkeley reunion. He took a deep breath, but no air seemed to come into his lungs.

He heard Graham come in over the headphones, his voice carrying concern. "You all right, Eric? Want to take a break?"

Eric waved his hand, then took another deep breath and counted in. He got to three before his kneecaps collided and thighs gave way, as if someone had dropped a stack of plywood on him. He gripped the microphone stand for support, but his hands slid down the steel pole. The last sight he saw was Graham pushing back his chair in the recording room with a startled look in his eyes.

He awoke in a bed, an IV in each arm. He figured out he was

in a hospital and then set about trying to deduce why he was there. He took a deep breath, felt a pain in his chest, and knew the world was different.

He lay in the dark, watching the sky outside gradually lighten, listening to the patter of nurses' shoes and the murmur of early-morning voices. A nurse came in, spoke to him, asking if he was comfortable. An hour later a young, pursed-lipped intern appeared. She stood beside the bed, holding her clipboard in front of her with both hands.

"How are you feeling?"

"Tired."

She nodded. "Do you know why you're here?"

"I suppose I'm more than just tired, right?"

She nodded again. "We found cancerous cells in your blood."

That would be those rotten lungs telling him his time was up.

"How bad is it?"

"We don't know. We need to run some tests this morning."

Ward and Lorraine arrived, her eyes swimming with worry. They were scheduled to leave that morning but Ward said he would stay and send Lorraine home. No, said Eric, he wasn't in the mood for someone hanging around, waiting for bad news. "I'll call if I need help. Whatever is going on down there in my lungs, I won't die tomorrow."

"Oh no, you'll call whether you need help or not. Tonight. You better, mister, or you'll be in serious trouble with me," said Lorraine.

"Okay."

"Tonight. We should get back about suppertime."

She looked at him accusingly. "Promise? Scout's honor?"

"Scout's honor."

She reached over and planted a kiss on his cheek. Ward shook his hand, using both of his hands, and then they left.

After a physical, X-rays, a sputum test, and a bronchoscopy, he returned to his bed. He filled out paperwork, watching the staff come and go. Eric saw hospitals as a theater that hosted one great choreography of death, the place where healthy cells at last succumb to those agents who have waited a lifetime to reign. A tech came by and brought him to the MRI center. When he returned, Graham was waiting in his room, uttering kind words. He left, saying he'd be back later in the day.

In the late afternoon, Eric made a trip to an oncologist's office. He got no surprises. The doctor was putting on his white coat when Eric came into his office. He wore an immaculately fitting wool suit. By its subtle shaping, smaller shoulders, and ticket pocket, Eric guessed it to be an Aquascutum or Burberry. How, Eric wondered, had he come to see the value in buying such expensive clothes? The doctor wore pair of Alden straight-tip blucher oxfords. Eric had an identical pair in his closet and could not help but wondering who would wear his shoes when he was gone.

Using X-rays, lab results, and MRI images, the oncologist explained that he had small-cell lung cancer. He said he could explain more when the cytology and pathology reports were complete, but that Eric must understand that the cancer was aggressive and had, in all likelihood, metastasized into his spine. Surgery would not be effective. Any treatment, even the most aggressive chemotherapy, was questionable.

"Your concerns now should concentrate on finding a place to rest and how to ameliorate pain," said the doctor.

"You mean finding a place to die."

"Yes. You've probably got six months or less."

———

WHEN THE cab pulled up to the curb, Eric saw Mr. Chou's daughter about to get into her car. She stopped when she saw Eric and waited for him to pay the driver.

When the cab sped away, she left her car door open and walked over to him and stood there with her hands at her side. "My father's not doing so well."

"Sorry. I haven't seen him out for a while."

She nodded. "He fell in the bathroom two weeks ago and fractured his hip. He can't get out of bed. He should be in a nursing home or hospice, but he won't go." She lifted her shoulders in resignation. "Just to let you know."

———

HE HADN'T been in the house for five minutes when the cell rang. It was Ward.

"Thought I was supposed to call you," said Eric.

"Lorraine is not in a waiting mood."

"I see."

"She wants to know if you're ready come back to Hake's Fork."

"I don't believe I have another hunt in me, Ward."

"That doesn't start until next September. We mean now."

"It might be a permanent visit."

Silence. "Damn. We were afraid of that, pilgrim. So sorry to hear that. So sorry."

"You still want me?"

"We're counting on it."

"How does Lorraine feel about this?"

"She talked about nothing else on the way home."

"How does Ward Fall feel about it?"

"We'll set you up in my office."

"I didn't ask for a plan of action. I asked how you felt about it," said Eric.

"Well, Lindsay. I'm still walking around with one last debt. Last month, you released me from a burden I've been carrying around for nearly thirty years."

"I believe there was a mutual shedding of burdens."

"Could be. But if your Nebraska girl were alive, she'd take care of you, wouldn't she? She was your biggest fan, you know."

"And I hers."

"Well, there you go. She's gone and we're here. The only kin you have is your mother and she's not exactly prospering. The bottom line is I'd feel a hell of lot better knowing you're not dying alone in that urban dung hole. So how about it?"

"I've got about a month's worth of work to do before I could come. You sure this is okay with Lorraine?"

"Do you require a written personal plea? She's got the whole thing planned, right down the meals."

"I'm favoring crackers and grapes these days, Ward."

"Crackers and grapes it is then, pilgrim."

———

ERIC LET his compositions consume him. Let the music take me before the worms or crematorium flames do, he thought each morning. He could not deny the disease, though. There was more blood in his spit and night sweats that left him drenched. He could only work about four hours at a stretch, then go home and sleep until the pain in his lungs woke him. Two days before Christmas he went to the studio to oversee one last mandolin fill, but found only Graham sitting at the console.

"Where's that kid you said would be here?"

"Told him not to come," said Graham.

"Why?"

"Listen to this, Eric."

Graham played back a movement that Eric called "Vineyard," written years back while watching Mexicans pick grapes. He imagined what the scene would look like from the eyes of a bird. One black-eyed gypsy, who executed a gracious choreography even while snipping clusters, and obviously had the affections of every male worker.

The movement had a mandolin player and the husky-voiced Lorraine on the vocal. He had told her: sing like the wind, this time, not water. A fall wind being chased by winter, he told her. Make no words, but just sing like the autumn wind. She loved his descriptions and improvised beautifully. It sounded good, but the tempo still lagged.

"Everybody's dragging the meter. We need to start from the beginning."

"The meter's fine," said Graham. "I warn you. The more you

dick with this number, the more flaws you're going to find. It's done."

"I still want to re-do it."

"Look, I tell you what, Lindsay. You let this sit for a week or ten days. Don't worry. Then give it another listen. If it still sounds slow, we'll pencil in another session. Right now, I think you need to take it easy."

CHAPTER 9

WARD INSISTED ON SETTING UP a hospital bed in his office. Eric fought the idea from inception. Nothing symbolized *infirm* like an articulated bed. Eventually he capitulated because he had less chest pain when sitting up. He'd been issued an oxygen tank, smaller than Mr. Chou's, and a slew of medicines, including methadone which tickled him, as if it were a tonic helping him withdraw from a habitual fighting of the world as it is.

The room held his final possessions: one drawerful of clothes, a few mystery novels, his Fender Rhodes, a Martin acoustic, and his dad's favorite fiddle. He packed his box of photo albums.

Mr. Chou had died on the second day of Chinese New Year. Eric had a freight company come and pack the Fender Rhodes. They shipped it to Hake's Fork. He sold all but two of his remaining instruments. Then he packed the trunk and back seat of the Porsche. The remainder of his belongings he left on the floor of the rental.

Against the advice of Ward and Lorraine and Graham, he had managed to drive the 911 all the way to Hake's Fork in late January and do so without incident. The night he arrived, he gave the keys to Josh, saying he didn't necessarily want them back. Josh just looked up at him, bug-eyed.

———

HIS WEIGHT dropped to below 110 for the first time since high school, and he had long stretches of nausea. The times he wasn't feeling wretched, he felt the best he'd ever felt in his life.

A week in Hake's Fork brought on the dreams. Portraits, faces especially, of those he'd known since young. It was as if he were flipping through a Rolodex of photos: Lester Sorensen, the tireless and steady drummer for Ray Lindsay and the Western Wheels; Ula at the sink, draining potatoes, her face turned in surprise at the camera; Danny Schwick, a frenetic tennis-crazy classmate from Valentine, stuck in a town with a single concrete court that gathered rainwater like a stopped gutter; Myra Finn, the counselor at Valentine Union High School who defended his right to wear a Nehru jacket at graduation. The images had a breathtakingly monochromatic durability, as if taken in dramatic light.

Eric recognized no common thread in the images until he saw in a flash that they were all images of energy expended. No moments of complacency. Each time, he awoke from having these dreams feeling as if he'd just been reacquainted with the people in the photographs. A yearning filled his bones and not for the first time he wondered if he was doing all the right things a person was supposed to do before they die.

One afternoon the twins trooped in, eager to share school photos. The images showed them dressed in identical striped blue-and-yellow western shirts that Lorraine had made.

"You want to put one of these up beside your bed?" asked Paul, holding out a photograph.

"Sure. Why not?" he said. "But where do I put them?"

"Dunno. Ask Mom. She'll figure something out," said Tim.

"Na-uh," said Paul. "Better ask Dad. He gets mad if we mess around in here."

Lorraine dug out a dusty bulletin board from storage. She hung it on the wall next to the bed and pinned on the photos of the boys.

"Looks empty," said Lorraine. "You need some more pictures, Eric."

"I don't have any."

"Well, don't be so helpless. Can't you do something about that? Didn't you bring along a box of pictures?"

"I have a few. How about you and Ward? Do you have any photos?"

Lorraine smiled widely, pleased that her hint was taken so quickly. "I suppose we could come up with something."

He awoke the next morning to find a photo of Ward, Lorraine, and the three boys wearing western-style snap shirts pinned up on the bulletin board. Lorraine suggested that he call up all those people he saw in his dreams and ask them for photographs of themselves. He dismissed it. Too much work. But as the days passed and the dreams continued, her idea seemed to resonate. He put the activity first on the day's agenda. Each morning, when his energy levels were at their highest, he'd telephone someone he'd seen in his dreams, someone who'd shown him affection or attention.

Alyson was incredulous and suspicious that he would want her picture and said no. Within a week, however, it arrived: a black-and-white taken on the set, pins in her mouth, adjusting the back of a woman's dress. Candice sent a picture of herself, her husband, and all four of the girls with a note: "For they, too, have loved you, Eric. They only know good things about you."

Slowly, the collection expanded with no refusals. The hard part was asking. The business about explaining his condition wearied him. Lorraine loved helping him with photos. This was her idea of fun. She went through his old photo albums: Graham, various musicians, a photo of his father playing the fiddle at a grange hall dance, laughing, laughing so hard it looked like the cigarette would fall from his mouth.

When it came to his mother, he posted a photo of her sitting on the front steps with Ula. Somewhere along the disposition line, there'd been a blatant distribution problem. Ula had gotten it all. Looks, faith, contentment, all the money she wanted, although her family lived modestly on her husband's salary as county road supervisor. His mother got the bilious nature and constant envy.

Yet, studying the photograph, he noticed, for the first time, the look of longing in both their eyes, a deep, ineffable yearning. Maybe Ula wasn't so content after all.

———

LATE IN the month he had a bad spell and barely had enough strength to walk to the bathroom. Letters blurred and danced before his eyes when he tried to read. The mere thought of calling for more photographs left him tired. Lorraine began reading to him after her morning chores. The sound of her voice gave him pleasure, the latent sing-song of her high German inflection coming to the forefront when she relaxed.

Words were not fast food for Lorraine. She understood that a book was not a radio manuscript and that an earnest reading, like slow-cooking a stew, rendered a richness not found in just spewing out information. Sometimes she read an article from a magazine, like *Reader's Digest*, sometimes from an older novel from Ward's collection, Turgenev or Hardy, but she also read the Bible to him for at least ten minutes daily. He didn't mind, just nothing too revelatory, he told her.

"Why not?"

"Too invasive."

"What the heck is that supposed to mean?" she said, a little defensively.

"Those apostles are so focused on revelation that they forget where the hell they are. That was Ula's problem. I've just figured this out, so bear with me. The prospect of heaven so excited her she'd forget she was still on earth. That's how she was killed, you know. One of the survivors of the accident said she was so enthralled explaining her interpretation of Revelation that she drove right through a red light and got creamed. The everyday was okay with her, but she needed something big to get excited. My mother was basically the same way. Me too, of course. Why should I be any different? I was always out there trying to pin down perfect. That's like trying to cinch down the end of the rainbow. There's always been a profound distrust in my mother's side of the here and now.

Matters had to be manipulated or be given a cosmic hue to be tolerable or be acceptable."

He stopped, out of breath, and took a series of short intakes of air from the oxygen tank.

"I want to stay here until I check out. I like sounds that help remind me of that, like the boys whipping by on their bicycles, riding in the mud, yelling their heads off, or chickens clucking, or that damned squeaking Powder River gate, or tractors rumbling by, and the heavenly smell of burning pine. Why would anyone want to leave that?"

She smiled as if she understood, although he wasn't quite sure.

"I like those words. They comfort me. But I guess I'm like your aunt. I'm so in love with Christ and his message that I can't help but ignore his promise of heaven. Although this place, this ranch, is a type of heaven, all right."

She paged through her worn Bible, then closed it, marking the place with her index finger. "Well, I was thinking about reading some Romans to you, but after what you said, I'm not sure you'd want it."

"No Romans for me." He laughed. "Ula loved Romans. She loved Paul's conviction that the travails of this world were worth it because heaven promised such glory."

Lorraine made a small murmuring sound of approval in the back of her throat. "But can't you see that Paul's testimony is about liberation? Eric, can you see that? In fact, aren't those his exact words, 'that creation will be liberated from its bondage'?"

She looked at him and smiled, then looked down in embarrassment. It was the first and only time she tried to change his mind about anything. He grabbed her hand.

"What I want," he said, almost breathless with emotion, "is not exact words. I want to know if I've paid back this life for what it's given me. Have I repaid my debt? Is there a chapter in the Bible that speaks to that? A passage that gives gratitude for the earthly. I've taken so much and given so little."

Lorraine drew back, puzzled, like a shy girl who's been asked to describe her own beauty. "Why, I don't know, Eric. I've never looked at life as a debt. So I've never asked the question or tried to find an answer in scripture. I can try if you like. But maybe that's something only you can answer. I don't know you really, but if you're anything like Ward, I bet you've packed around a debt that would flatten a mule. We do just what we can do, that's what I tell Ward. And sometimes that includes a lot of mistakes."

He nodded as if the words assuaged some pain. "Please read to me."

"Okay. What do you want?"

"Robert Louis Stevenson."

"Not *Treasure Island* again?"

"No. *Kidnapped*. Now there's a story about real liberation."

HE OCCASIONALLY perused Ward's library, but left the philosophy books untouched. One evening when Ward came in to check on him, Eric asked, "Do you ever re-read these books, Fall?"

"Most of them, no."

"Then why keep them?"

"Oh, I don't know. I guess because I can't stop asking those questions that are past cliché yet somehow keep being asked. You know: why does the world treat us as it does? Do we choose our own world? And so forth. Want to expose the boys."

"Expose them to what?"

Ward grinned and pulled out a copy of Bertrand Russell's *A History of Western Philosophy*. "Remember this guy? Knocked my socks off that someone could put it all into one volume. A confirmed pessimist, though."

He reshelved the book. "I'm just the opposite. I keep hoping these books will tell me something I don't already know, that someday I'll develop enough...wisdom to gain new appreciation for what they're saying."

Eric mustered up all this strength and propped himself up in bed. His head throbbed with irritation. "Fall. You're not serious. You're spouting a form of Hake's Fork humor, right?"

Ward shook his head, looking a little sheepish. "No, not really."

"Christ, Ward. You've gained enough wisdom in your lifetime to supplant three generations of philosophers. Or at least sit at the table with the sages. You've died, or accepted your death, and now choose to live. What greater wisdom is there? How many of these men who wrote all these grand books have done what you did with their own lives? Nary a single fucking one. Now stop hoping there's something better. That was my disease. Look where I am. Do you know how much Kant and Hegel would envy you? Jung would do fucking handsprings. What was that line you gave me while hunting, 'It's a deep sickness that you've got to think smart.' Didn't you say that? So don't implant the standards of these books on your kids."

Eric flopped down on the bed, exhausted, and grabbed the oxygen mask.

"Well now," said Ward, looking at him, grinning. "With that sort of conviction you'll live at least another year."

"Sorry," said Eric, after a few intakes from the mask, "that was a little preachy, wasn't it?"

"'Sall right. You're right."

Eric took one more huff of oxygen then sat up again. "Look, on to more practical matters. As you would say: here's the deal. I know you and Lorraine have been wondering what to do with my body when I'm gone. How about I get buried here?"

"Where?"

"Someplace along the bottom."

Ward smiled. "You mean someplace where we can drive a backhoe."

"I've always wanted to operate a backhoe, Ward."

"What person with a pecker doesn't?"

They both laughed. Eric's chest ached almost unbearably.

"I can't ask someone else to dig my own grave."

"Anything you want, pilgrim. Let me know if you want help. I better discuss this with Lorraine before I give the okay."

"Of course. And if you want to put a headstone on my grave, fine. People may want to know where I'm buried. Maybe one of my ex-wives. But Ward, I've got no real kin left. When my mother dies, you take up the headstone. I want no separation between me and this earth."

OUR MAN from Valentine, who once feared boomerangs, most self-launched, now rests, half sitting, half lying down, with the ultimate boomerang ominously pitched over his head. He's laughing at it, snapping rubber bands at it, sometimes paperclips, occasionally phonebooks and magazines when he's lit on methadone, taken for a pain that drives him down like a miner's drill.

He spent one afternoon watching the icicles fall, one by one, off the barn roof.

"Bleak March, awful damned season," declares his host, but Eric doesn't complain. He's got his piano. He plays old Beatles songs for the boys when his energy level obliges. Sometimes he plays his own CD. It still sounds good. Thin as a curtain rod, he nibbles at homemade toast covered with butter and sweetened juneberry preserves. Pretzels taste pretty good. He wears clothes purchased at the Salvation Army.

Then warmth and clear weather in April. He doesn't feel any better, but one last plateau gives him relief for a few days. The ground dries enough for Ward to drill in a crop of spring wheat. He even lets Eric drive the tractor as he is so exhausted from late calving that he needs time to catch up on sleep. Eric marvels at hearing the meadowlark above the roar of the tractor. What determination to be heard!

His hosts check on him that night and he tells them to go back to bed for God's sake, he won't expire before dawn. The next morning rain pounds on the study roof and he plays jigs on his dad's fiddle. Short tunes. The notes come as easily as they did when he played them thirty years ago with the Western Wheels when they did gigs in O'Neill County. The old Irish would come out of the woodwork, get out on the floor and stomp like Goliath, floor joists quaking.

After playing two or three jigs, he collapses back ono his bed, exhausted, and thinks a glass of Jameson would taste divine, but knows there's some things you shouldn't go back on, even when avowals don't matter much anymore.

———

WARD AND Lorraine sat in the kitchen drinking coffee. The discussion on what to do about the Porsche parked in their shed had turned mildly adversarial. Lorraine wanted to sell it immediately and even suggested putting an advertisement in the local want ads that morning. Ward counseled deliberation and said that, besides, it was Josh's vehicle and he needed an active role in determining the car's future.

Ward heard the backhoe start up. He stopped with his cup halfway between the table and his mouth, then slowly took a sip. Lorraine looked at him.

"Do you suppose he'll be all right?" she asked, using the same tone as the one she used about Timothy or Paul on a new horse or Josh with his learner's permit. Then she smiled, a small grin, really, at the nature of her own questions. Their guest made few demands. Coffee. Toast. Occasionally bananas. Basically the diet of Minky. Except Minky did not smoke, and Eric still did.

Ward went to the window and watched the yellow backhoe disappear over the hilltop. Legal questions came, then slid away. Eventually, people would come asking what had happened to Eric Lindsay. He would deal with that when the time came. The rules governing the dead had always been slippery in this country.

———

THE LEVERS on the backhoe were like keys and pedals on a piano: moving, shifting, touching, squeezing a movement. The work was mostly mental—where to extend, when to retract. Listening to the rising and dipping of the engine, the backhoe felt like a rowboat tied up to a dock in choppy water. The sod, soft from spring rain, offered little resistance.

———

THE DAY after he dug his grave, he had a final burst of energy and carried the fiddle down to the alfalfa flats, dressed in a T-shirt and sweatpants. He played and whirled but after five minutes sank to his knees and retched all over the inch-high alfalfa, just starting to poke its head among the timothy and brome. His hosts helped him back to bed.

———

LORRAINE HELD vigil, but she had nodded off when he died, seed catalog in her lap. Ward came in a little after midnight from checking on Blue Sky. She was due to foal any day now. A power outage left only light from a kerosene lantern. While his skin was ashen and shrunken, Eric's eyes remained so shiny they reflected the lantern's flame.

At his request, they used no coffin. Instead they wrapped Eric's body in his elk hide. Over the winter, Lorraine had cured the hide to a malleable softness. Ward speculated that the hide wouldn't be sufficient to cover him. The cow wasn't that large. But, small in stature anyway, Eric had withered to nothing.

Lorraine went to the house and made a pot of coffee. She returned with the full pot and two cups. Ward watched as she expertly trimmed the hide to it fit around his body and stitched him up with rawhide strand like a papoose, hair side in. He held the hide, watching Eric's face disappear, his eyes bright to the last. Over Lorraine's objections, Ward kept the eyes open. He wanted those bright orbs peeking out, curious and relaxed, to be his last vision of Eric Lindsay.

As they were finishing up, light creeping in the windows, Josh cautiously slid into the study door, hair matted by sleep, dressed in pajama top, blue jeans, and Nikes with no socks.

He hesitated, then whispered. "He's gone, isn't he? I mean he's dead."

"Yes, he is. Would you help me bury him? Why don't you get a coat first?" said Ward.

Josh and Ward carried the body and slid it into the back of the truck.

"Boy, he doesn't weigh much more than a bale of hay, does he?" said Josh.

Lorraine stood beside the truck watching, her eyes moist. When Eric first arrived, she'd spent many evening in tears. Now she seemed cried out. In one last gesture, she reached out and touched the fringe of the elk hide. "You two go on. The twins will be awake soon. Breakfast will be ready when you return."

The tires rolled on wet ground. A magpie croaked from the branch of a crooked ponderosa pine above the house, its feathers ruffled by a warm east wind, the first of the year, kindled from the heat of the prairie.